Neykoota

Forgotten

Olympia Publishers
London

www.olympiapublishers.com
OLYMPIA PAPERBACK EDITION

Copyright © Neykoota 2022

The right of Neykoota to be identified as author of
this work has been asserted in accordance with sections 77 and 78
of the Copyright, Designs and Patents Act 1988.

All Rights Reserved

No reproduction, copy or transmission of this publication
may be made without written permission.
No paragraph of this publication may be reproduced,
copied or transmitted save with the written permission of the
publisher, or in accordance with the provisions
of the Copyright Act 1956 (as amended).

Any person who commits any unauthorised act in relation to
this publication may be liable to criminal
prosecution and civil claims for damage.

A CIP catalogue record for this title is
available from the British Library.

ISBN: 978-1-80074-264-2

This is a work of fiction.
Names, characters, places and incidents originate from the writer's
imagination. Any resemblance to actual persons, living or dead, is
purely coincidental.

First Published in 2022

Olympia Publishers
Tallis House
2 Tallis Street
London
EC4Y 0AB

Printed in Great Britain

Dedication

To those who stood by me through thick and thin, thank you.

Chapter One

As I walked through the coffee house's door, the strong smell of coffee filled my lungs. It was eight in the morning so it was crowded and it would take at least fifteen minutes to get a cup of coffee. You might think that I could just drink some coffee at home but if I have a long stressful day like today, I prefer not to worry about making coffee.

As I got to the front of the line, I ordered a large cup of black coffee and a slice of double chocolate cake. I had to last till noon since I had a pain in the ass class with an old son of a bitch who's always making fun of everyone. But thankfully it was the last class of the semester.

I grabbed my cup and cake and paid but as I was about to walk out of the door, I noticed my old high school friend, James. I hadn't seen him in about two years. We stayed in touch the summer after he graduated but then we drifted apart as Ben, my brother, left for college. I've only been in touch with him through social media; but to be honest, I don't consider that staying in touch. I don't know a damn thing about him nowadays. I think it's more my fault than it's his. I stayed away from so many people after I went through a dark depression two years ago; and that included James, too.

He was sitting in a corner, talking to some girl who was clearly still drunk from last night. At first, I just wanted to say hi but then I changed my mind. I decided to scare the girl away.

Maybe she would learn the listen that talking to strangers when she's still drunk in the morning is not a good idea.

"Oh, hey baby! Thanks for meeting me here. Good news. I'm pregnant!" I said it in the most dramatic way I possibly could.

The girl just got up and left. Fortunately, she didn't have any coffee left in her cup and couldn't throw it in his face. I sat down as she walked out of the door.

"Wow! You still got it!" he said.

"And you still hit on poor drunk girls," I said and laughed.

We both laughed and got up and hugged each other. It's been so long since the last time I'd seen him.

"Oh, I've missed you so much!" he said as he was squeezing me so hard.

"Me too!" I said as I was in his arms.

"Going to class?" he asked as we sat down.

"Yeah. How did you know?" I asked curiously.

"First of all, you would never wake up this early if you don't have to. And secondly because of your outfit. Oh, and you're carrying a bunch of stuff," he said and took a sip from his cup with a proud look on his face.

Well, he was not wrong. It's no secret that I've never been a morning person and my outfit was simple and comfortable. I was wearing a pair of dark navy-blue jeans, a white knitted sweater, a navy-blue coat with a pair of chocolate boots. I just laughed in return.

"Your class is at nine?" he asked and I nodded.

"So, we should get going if you don't want to be late," he said and got up.

"What?" I asked confused.

As he got up, I noticed that he had his guitar with him.

"I have a class at nine, too. We can walk to the campus together," he said and walked out.

"You go to NYU?" I asked like it was the biggest question in the world.

"Well, yeah! Didn't you know?" he asked.

"Hell no!" I said.

"Well, that explains a lot!" he said.

"You thought that I was ignoring you? Oh, James! I would never ignore you! I'm just really busy," I said with guilt.

"Yeah, I know. You're like the most famous person in NYU right now," he said.

I blushed immediately. I really didn't know that. I really didn't know anything happening around the campus. I'm always coming and going. I never spent any of my spare time there. If I have any time to myself I would either sleep or go out with my boyfriend, Nick.

"But how come I had never seen you there?" I asked.

"If you get your head out of your phone, you'd see me all the time," he said and I got embarrassed.

We walked to the campus together and James told me a little about well, me! He said there was even an article about my last gallery in the school's paper. Apparently, everybody knows who I am.

The morning passed pretty fast which I didn't expect. My class was done and everybody had left the classroom and I was grabbing my last pieces to go when Bella, my assistant, called.

"Hey boss! How's everything?" she asked as I picked up.

"Fine. Is everything ready for the meeting with The Young's?" I asked.

"Yeah, everything is ready. I had emailed you all the photos of your collection so you don't have to take twenty-five paintings with you to the meeting," she said.

"Okay! Thank you," I said.

"Oh, and the meeting is in their downtown office so you might want to get out of your apartment a little sooner. There might be traffic. Do you want me to come with you?" she asked.

"No, I'm good. Just sent me the certain location of it," I said.

"Okay! Good luck there!" she said.

I hung up and grabbed my stuff and walked out of the classroom. As soon as I walked out of the door, I bumped into someone and all of my stuff dropped from my hands.

"I am so sorry!" he said as he knelt down to help me pick them up.

"It's fine," I said.

As I picked up all of my stuff and looked up, I saw the most beautiful pair of green eyes in the world. It just took my breath away. They looked so familiar, like I had seen them before somewhere but I couldn't quite remember where.

I looked away as soon as I could. I just got up and left. I was about to walk out the door when someone called me. As I turned around, I saw James with the green-eyed guy. He was tall and handsome as hell. He had light brown hair with some pieces in his face, driving more attention to his eyes. He had a gentle smile of his face.

"I didn't know you were still here," James said.

"Yeah, I usually get out sooner than this," I said and tried not to look at his friend.

"Yeah! I know!" he said.

"Don't you want to introduce us?" the green-eyed guy asked.

"Well, this is the one and only Miss Brooke Edwards and this is my very good friend, Charles Young," James said and we shook hands.

"Nice to meet you!" he said.

"You too!" I said.

We locked eyes for a few second as my hand was still in his.

"We were going to get some lunch. Do you want to join us?" James asked.

"Oh, I'd loved to but I need to get ready for an important meeting," I said.

"Big exhibition coming up?" Charles asked.

"Yeah! Somehow my biggest yet," I said.

"Isn't it tomorrow?" James asked.

I just nodded. Before any of us could say anything, my phone rang and it was Bella again. Suddenly I got a bad feeling that it was bad news.

"Sorry I got to take this. It was really nice meeting you," I said and left.

"What's up Bella? Did anything bad happen?" I asked as I picked up.

"God, no! Take a deep breath. You're going to give yourself a heart attack! I just called to say that there is a slight change of plans. Mister Young cannot make it for the meeting so there will be his son in the meeting," she said.

I let out a deep breath as I heard that nothing has gone wrong till now. I hoped nothing else happens at the last minute.

"Okay! Thanks for calling," I said.

As I was walking home, I ordered lunch so when I get home, I wouldn't have to wait so long. I was starving. Ever though I ate more than I usually eat for breakfast, I was pretty hungry. A few minutes after I got home, my lunch arrived. I ate and took a shower. I straightened my hair and tied it into a high ponytail. I did a natural makeup. I didn't want it to be too much. I needed to look serious for this meeting.

The Young's has been one of the best customers I had over the last few months so when they asked to if they could see the collection before the exhibition, I just said yes. It was a charity exhibition so it was pretty important to me to sell all of my paintings. Not that all of my last collections haven't gone sold out in two days but it was a one-night exhibition and the charity needed the money.

It was nearly four o'clock so I just got dressed. I wore a black dress that was long enough to cover my knees. I didn't want the scar on my leg to show. It had semi long sleeves and a low-neckline. I matched it with a pair of red high heels and a gray overcoat. Before I grabbed my purse and other stuff, I called a cab.

It took me about forty minutes to get there. The meeting was at five and I arrived there a little bit earlier. I was pretty nervous. I stood there, in front of that beautiful white building and thought about my presentation for one last time.

It was getting late so I took my last deep breath and went in. As I was waiting for the elevator, someone came and stood by my side. I could say it was a man from his cologne and the sound of his strong steps. I didn't care enough to look and see his face. If it was someone who knew me, he would say something.

The elevator came and we got in. My head was hanging low, going through everything for the last time on my iPad. I just pressed the eighth floor's button. He didn't press anything. After a few seconds, as the elevator stopped and the doors opened, he talked.

"After you Miss Edwards," he said and let me leave first.

I was shocked. It was Charles, James's friend. I was in shock for some time but then I pulled myself back together and walked out. I gave him a little smile and headed to the conference room where the meeting was supposed to be. Everybody was already there. So, I said hi to everyone and got ready for my presentation. Mister Young's seat was still empty, waiting for his son to arrive.

I took off my overcoat and straightened my dress. I set up my stuff and connected my iPad to the projector. I was ready to start but Mister Young's seat was still empty.

After five minutes or so, Charles walked into the conference room, said hello to everyone and sat in Mister Young's seat. I was shocked. Charles Young was Mister Young's son? I was in shock for a while even after I started my presentation.

"First of all, thank you for having me. This collection means a lot to me and like I said before I'm going to donate all of my earnings to the charity so more children can have a better education and the chance to follow their dreams," I said.

I was still pretty nervous and stressed out when I started. But after about ten minutes or so I could pull myself back together. As my presentation ended, they took a closer look at my collection. It was nothing I did before. They had a surrealism and a bit of expressionism vibe when my last two collections were completely cubism.

"I have to say, Miss Edwards, your entire collection is amazing," Charles said a few minutes after my presentation ended.

"Thank you!" I said.

"I was wondering if we could buy your entire collection," he said.

Everyone in the room turned around and looked at him in disbelief. I heard a few gasped. No one including myself could believe it. Charles just kept his eyes on me and was waiting for my response. I kept my face straight when I hardly could hide the way he surprised me. I wasn't even sure I had heard him right. But the way everyone was looking at him showed I had heard him right.

"It would be my honor!" I said.

I couldn't believe that I said it so calmly. But as I said it, everyone turned and stared at me with their mouths hung open. But I didn't even look at them. My eyes were on that handsome green-eyed man across the table.

We shook hands and they told me they will bring the contract to the gallery tomorrow morning. I thanked them and walked out of the door. As I was waiting for the elevator to come up, Charles came and stood by me again. We didn't say a thing in the hallway but as we got in and the doors closed, he spoke up.

"Would you join me for a toast?" he asked.

"You know I'm eighteen, right?" I asked in return.

"Who said anything about celebrating in public? James would be happy to see you," he asked.

"As much as I've missed him I can't. I have plans with my boyfriend," I said.

The gentle smile on his face faded and he didn't say another word. As we got out of the elevator and we were walking out of the building, my phone rang. It was Nick so I picked up quickly.

"Hey! Are you on your way?" I asked.

"Hi. No! I got stuck at work. Sorry baby. I'll make it up to you," he said.

"It's okay," I said and hung up.

It really bummed me out. We haven't seen each other for like ten days now and he cancels on me like this; at the last minute?

"Is everything all right?" Charles asked.

I didn't even notice he was still there. I though he must be gone but he wasn't.

"Yeah, no! My dear boyfriend just called and told me that he's stuck at work," I said.

He could hear how pissed I was. Ten days is a long time not to see your boyfriend or girlfriend. How could he do this? Couldn't he do his work a little quicker so he wouldn't have to stay late in the office?

"I'm sorry. Would you come over now? I mean if you like to," he asked.

"Yeah, sure!" I said with a smile.

Chapter Two

As we walked into their apartment, James pulled me in his arms and hugged me tightly.

"Oh, I'm so glad that you came!" he said as I was still in his arms.

"I had plans with my boyfriend but he canceled on me at the last minute so yeah, I came!" I said.

Charles went straight to his room after saying hi to James. I pulled away from his arms and he led me to the living room. It was a small apartment but it was enough for two guys. It was pretty clean, unexpectedly. We sat down on the couch and James stared at me to start talking but I didn't.

"So, how was the last two years of high school?" he asked since I didn't say a thing.

"Horrible!" I said and rolled my eyes.

"Why? What happened?" he asked with a straight face.

"Lots of stuff had happened. All of those girls who were always around me and hanging out with me disappeared. They were only hanging out with me because they had a crush on you or Ben or sometimes both. I got so lonely that I left the cheerleading team. And then things got worse and worse from there," I said with a little smile which was pretty fake.

His eyes saddened. The smile on his face disappeared completely. Before he could say a world, Charles came out of his room. He had changed into something more comfortable than his suit. He was wearing a pair of black jeans and a bright yellow hoodie. As Charles came, James didn't say a thing.

"What should we eat? I was thinking I'd cook something!" Charles said as he sat on the single couch.

"Yeah! That would be amazing," James said.

I just got surprised that he could cook. I mean most of the guys don't know how to cook and rich guys like Charles do not cook. At least not the ones I know.

"So, I was thinking lasagna. Is it good?" Charles asked.

"It's perfect!" I said with a goofy smile.

I had feeling that he knew it was my favorite food. James must have told him. Charles left James and I alone and went to the kitchen.

"I'm so sorry. I really didn't know!" he said.

We talked for a little while before my feet started to hurt in my high heels so I just took them off. I crossed my right leg over my left. It made my dress go a little up and reveal my scar. I tried to cover it before James would see it but he did see it before I could cover it up.

"What was that?" he asked with a worried look in his eyes.

"It's nothing," I said like nothing happened.

But it did happen. He didn't know because my father didn't let anyone find out that I was driving when I was drunk and didn't have a driver's license.

"Brooke? The last time I saw you, you didn't have a scar on your leg. What happened?" he asked again.

I knew he wouldn't give it up. Even though I wasn't really comfortable to talk about it, I had to tell him. He was getting more worried and anxious every second.

"Okay! Umm, last winter I was home alone and I started

drinking. Before I knew it, I was drunk. I had just broken up with my ex-boyfriend and I was mad at him for some reasons that I still cannot remember. I took the keys to one of my father's cars and drove. I wanted to go to his place. But I never got there. I got into an accident," I said and took a deep breath to keep my tears from falling.

He gave me a tissue to wipe my tears before it could ruin my makeup.

"After the accident, I was in coma for twenty days. And when I woke up, I couldn't remember a thing. It took me a month to get my memories back by reading my dairies and a therapist. But still, I cannot remember the last month before the accident. All I know about it is that something horrible happened and I couldn't even write about it in my journals," I said and took another deep breath.

"And on top of these all, after I got out of coma and got my memories back, I wanted to talk to Ben but he ignored me. I don't even know why. I just wanted to talk to him, but he wouldn't answer my calls. He wouldn't call me back. I knew he knew what happened the night of my birthday but..." I couldn't say another word.

I wanted to let go and let the tears wash over my face. I wanted to cry my eyes out but I couldn't. Not only because it would make James even more worried than he already was but because of Charles. I met him just a couple of hours ago. I couldn't cry in front of him.

James pulled me in his arms and held me close for a little while. He was playing with me ponytail as I was in his arms and it drew my attention away from the accident.

"Brooke, you know you can tell me anything right?" he asked.

"I know!" I said and he kissed my forehead.

"Promise me you will never hide anything from me ever again," he said.

"I promise!" I said.

"Go wash you face before the tears burn you face," he said and kissed my forehead again.

I grabbed my purse and went to their guest bathroom. My makeup was ruined, especially my eye makeup. I looked like a panda. I grabbed a makeup removal wipe from my purse and removed my makeup. I untied my ponytail and let my hair fall on my back. As I opened the door, I heard them talking but then I froze as I heard them talking about me.

"Brooke is a grown independent woman. You shouldn't be worried about her this much!" Charles said.

"I know. But I can't get it out of my head that if I had been around nothing would happen to her," James said.

A tear dropped on my cheek and I wiped it quickly. I took a deep breath and went to the kitchen. Charles was nearly done with the lasagna but I asked if I could help anyway.

"If you could grate the cheese, it would be awesome," he said.

I nodded with a smile and he gave me the grater and the cheese sticks. I washed my hands and started to grate. As I was finished, I gave him the bowl of cheese.

We sat in the kitchen for a while and talked till the diner was ready. Charles sat the table and picked out a bottle of red wine. It was at least ten years old. A few minutes before he wanted to take out the lasagna out of the oven, my phone rang. It was Nick. So, I went to the living room to pick up.

"Hi honey. How are you?" he said as I picked up.

"I'm fine," I said coldly. I was still mad at him.

"I'm so sorry about tonight. I still couldn't get out of the office. Do want me to come over after I'm done here?" he asked.

There was something different in his voice, like he was just pretending to care. Before I could say anything, Charles called me.

"Brooke, I'm taking the lasagna out of the oven. Are you coming?" he said loudly.

"What the hell was that?" Nick shouted in my ear.

"I'm at my friends' house," I said calmly, ignoring his rage.

"Yeah, like you have any friends!" he said with anger and sarcasm.

"What the hell is that supposed to mean?" I asked with rage.

"Don't lie to me. You don't have any friends!" he said even louder that hurt my ear drum.

It was kind of true. I didn't have many friends. But Nick didn't know about the few I had.

"Maybe if you had spent more time with me, you'd know!" I said louder than him.

I didn't wait for him to say another word. I just hung up on him. I turned off my phone and left in the living room. As I sat down, James looked at me with worried eyes. He must have heard the way Nick rose his voice at me. I'm not going to lie. It wasn't pretty seeing your oldest girlfriend being screamed at. He had every right to be worried about me right now.

Charles took the lasagna out of the oven and put it right in the middle of the table. He opened the wine and poured a glass for everyone and sat down.

"A toast to Brooke and her amazing new collection!" Charles said as he rose his glass.

We drank a toast and started to eat. I couldn't believe that he really cooked that lasagna. It was amazing. I wished I could eat more but I really couldn't. It was a pretty heavy meal for me.

As we were eating, we mostly talked about NYU and what we are eventually going to do. I didn't know why but I was one hundred present sure that I had seen Charles somewhere but I didn't know where or when, yet. Maybe I had seen him in the period of time I can't remember. But yet if we had met in that period of time, he would say something but he didn't.

They told me about their charity concert on Sunday. They were planning it for months now. It was a bunch of juniors and a few seniors. They were so exited since they had invited a few journalists and bloggers to their performance. It could change everybody's lives and they hoped it would.

When we all ate, we left the dishes in the sink and Charles put the left overs in the fridge. We each grabbed our glasses and went to the living room. We drank until the second bottle was empty. It was getting late. I wanted to go home. I needed to get some proper sleep especially after all those drinks we've had.

"I think I better get going! I have a pretty busy day tomorrow," I said.

"I can give a ride," Charles said casually.

"Thank you!" I said with a smile.

Before he could say anything else, his phone rang.

"I'm sorry I should take this but after that I'll take you home!" he said.

"Okay!" I said.

Charles grabbed his phone and went to his bedroom. He wasn't drunk at all. I wondered how many glasses of wine could get him drunk.

I knew James would say something any minute about who was on the phone and why was he raising his voice at me. And as soon as we were alone, he began.

"Who the hell was that?" he asked with rage.

"It was my dear boyfriend!" I said and rolled my eyes.

"Why was he talking to you like that?" he asked.

"When Charles said that dinner was ready, he heard him and got angry when I'm the one who should have been angry at him. We haven't seen each other in like ten days and he canceled on me at the last minute. Now he's mad because I didn't go home to an empty apartment and I came here and hang out with you guys," I said and let out a sad sigh.

"Are you okay? I mean you and him!" He asked.

"Not really. We are both really busy and don't see each other much. He knew how busy I am when he first asked me out. But for the last month all I heard was complains and now when I clear some time to see him, he freaking cancels at the last minute," I said sadly.

"Do you love him?" he asked.

"I liked him at first but now I don't even think that I like him anymore!" I said and leaned back on the couch.

"Does he feel the same?" he asked.

"I really don't know! But I think we can't do anything for our relationship anymore. I mean when he accused me of cheating, what can I do?" I asked.

"Why would he do that?" he asked confused.

"When I said I'm at my friends' house, he accused me of

lying and said that I don't have any friends! What does he know? He barely spends any time with me and now he expects to know my friends? Such a bastard!" I said and rolled my eyes.

"So, if you are not in love with him and you don't even like him anymore as you said and he's treating you like this, why don't you break up with him? He clearly doesn't deserve a wonderful girl like you," he said.

He was right. I think I was so busy these last couple of weeks that I really couldn't think about my relationship with Nick. I should break up with him sooner rather than later. Maybe tomorrow morning? Should I call him or text him or do it in person? I'll figure it out tomorrow when I'm sober.

"Yeah, I should end it. I think I was just too busy that I didn't have any time to think about our relationship!" I said.

I knew it was the right thing to do for both of us. Nick is too proud to admit that it was a mistake from the beginning but I'm not. I had to end it as soon as possible.

James opened his mouth to say something but as his phone rang, he didn't say a word. As he looked at the caller ID, he smiled. It must have been someone especial that made James, the player smiled widely.

"Sorry Brooke! I got to take this," he said and went to his room.

And I was left alone in the living room. I was pretty tired and Charles hasn't come back so I just rested my head on the back of the couch and closed my eyes. I didn't even notice when I fell asleep.

Chapter Three

"I'm sorry I should take this but after that I'll take you home!" I said and went to my bedroom.

My dad was calling me and I knew for sure it was about the meeting and possibly about me buying her whole collection.

"Hi Dad! How's London?" I asked as I picked up.

"Hey son! Is it true that you bought Miss Edwards' whole collection?" he asked in shock.

"Yeah!" I said with a little laughter.

"I'm just curious, why would you do that?" He laughed and asked.

"Because it was amazingly good?" I asked.

He just laughed and didn't say anything at first.

"Are you sure it didn't have anything to do with her cuteness?" he asked.

"Dad! Stop!" I said with objection.

"What? You'd be blind not to see it!" he said it to tease me.

"I do see it but it's not the reason that I bought her whole collection. It was just so amazing. I couldn't resist," I said honestly.

"All right. Whatever you say son!" he said.

"Who even told you that? Samantha?" I asked.

She must have told him. After all she's his assistant. She

tells him every single thing that happens around the company. She knows everything and everyone.

"Well, I called Samantha to see how the meeting went and she told me a lot of things," he said.

"Oh my God! What did she tell you?" I asked.

She was a smart woman. I was pretty sure she noticed the way I was looking at Brooke the entire meeting. She's unfairly fair. Anyone who couldn't see it was definitely blind.

"She told me how you got so suited up for her and how you couldn't look away from her the entire time!" he said with laughter.

I got embarrassed. It was true. I usually don't suit up but for especial occasions I do.

"Well, that's true! But I can't make a move right now! She has a boyfriend," I said.

I somehow knew she has a boyfriend. In her last exhibitions I saw her with a guy and he wouldn't leave her side. He had numb eyes and I couldn't see anything in his eyes. Or maybe I was just jealous because he had her and I didn't.

"So, you already asked her out!" he said and laughed.

I didn't know why my dad was laughing so much about this but it was somehow fun to hear him talk about his son's love life like this. I didn't mind it. Anything that made him laugh was worth it. We didn't see or hear him laugh much after my mom passed away. So, if making fun of the way I'm so into Brooke makes him laugh, then let it be it.

"No dad! It just came up," I said.

"And how exactly it came up? By asking her out?" he asked with curiosity.

"I invited her back to our place to celebrate and she said that she had plans with her boyfriend," I said.

"Oh! I'm sorry!" he said.

"Oh no. She's here. That jerk canceled on her at the last minute!" I said somehow happily.

"So why are you talking to me?" he asked.

"Because you called me," I said and laughed.

"Okay! Now go. We can talk latter," he said.

We said goodbye and hung up. When I got back to the living room, she had fallen asleep. I couldn't wake her up. She was sleeping so peacefully. I put her legs up on the couch and covered her with a soft warm blanket. I wasn't tired so I just went to the kitchen to do the dishes. After a while James came, too.

"When did Brooke fall asleep?" he asked.

"I don't know! She was asleep when I came back," I said.

"How was the meeting?" he asked.

"Pretty good!" I said.

"How good?" he asked.

"So good that I bought her whole collection," I said.

The dishes were done so I washed my hands and dried them. I leaned back against the counter to face James. He was still processing what I just said.

"You bought her entire collection?" he asked.

"Well, yeah!" I said like it was not a big deal.

"Why would you do that?" he asked with laughter.

"Because it was good! I just couldn't resist," I said.

"You couldn't resist it or you couldn't resist her?" he asked with a huge smirk on his face.

"Oh, Shut up!" I said.

"Okay!" I said, trying to end the conversation.

"You're so falling for her!" he said with a huge smile on his face.

"Maybe! I don't know. She's something special. But she has a dickhead boyfriend," I said.

I was pretty pissed at him. Who would cancel on their girlfriend like that at the last minute? Only jerks do that and of course cheaters. He doesn't know what a great girl he has.

"Maybe in few days she won't have a dickhead boyfriend anymore!" he said with a smirk.

"Why would you say that?" I asked with curiosity.

"She wants to break up with him," he said with his happy smile.

"No! She's not!" I said in shock.

"Yes, she will!" he said.

The way he was certain about it made me happy. He truly didn't deserve her.

"But even if she breaks up with him tomorrow, I can't make a move for at least another month," I said.

"You're not proposing to her! You're asking her out," he said like I was overthinking it, which I was.

But he wasn't wrong. I could wait a few days and see what happens then.

"Okay!" I said.

"Do you think I should wake her up?" I asked after a few minutes of silence.

"No, just let her sleep. She was so tired," he said.

I just nodded. We went to our bedrooms to get some sleep. I wasn't really tired so I couldn't sleep. But mostly I couldn't get Brooke out of my head. I couldn't and I wouldn't deny how much I liked her. It was undeniable. Ever since her first exhibition, I knew I liked her. She was fair, talented, independent, smart. Who wouldn't want to be with her? Who wouldn't want to love her as much as they could?

When I went to her first exhibition, I was expecting an spoiled rich girl who thought she was Leonardo de Vinci. But as I walked in there, I got amazed. She was amazingly talented. I think most of the people who went to her first exhibition expected the same thing as I did. But she proved everybody that she was an amazing independent woman with amazing talents.

An hour passed by and I couldn't sleep. I got up to get some water. But as I opened the door, I heard a weak crying sound. I couldn't tell where it was coming from. I went to the living room to check on Brooke, in case it was hers. It was hers. She was still asleep but her face was covered in tears. I tried to wake her up but she wouldn't open her eyes. I put my hand on her shoulder and shook her. After a few minutes she woke up but it didn't look good. She was looking at me like a stranger.

"Brooke? Are you all right?" I asked.

"Where am I? Who are you?" she asked.

"You don't remember?" I asked.

She shook her head no. I got scared. She was looking around, probably to figure out where she was. I was freaking out. I didn't know what to do. She was shaking so badly so I reached for the blanket to cover up her with it. She got scared and backed out. She was probably more scared than I was, waking up in a guy's apartment and not remembering anything. She must be terrified.

"It's okay. I just want to cover you with the blanket. It seems like you're cold!" I manage to say it calmly when I was still freaking out.

She nodded and let me cover her shoulders with the blanket. She stopped shaking after a while but still couldn't remember a thing. I went to the kitchen to get a glass of water for her. But first I drank a glass of ice-cold water myself.

"Here. Have some water. I'll be right back," I said as I gave her the glass of water.

She just nodded in return. She was still looking at me like a stranger. I was really freaking out so I just did the only thing I could think of. I went to James's room and woke him up.

"James? Wake up. I need you," I said.

"What?" he asked as he rubbed his eyes.

"Umm, how should I say this? Brooke was crying in her sleep so I woke her up and now she cannot remember where she is or who I am!" I said trying my best to stay calm.

"What do you mean she can't remember where she is or who you are?" he asked as he got up.

"She can't remember a thing, James! She didn't tell you anything about it? Is it some sort of illness?" I asked.

"I have no clue," he said.

As we went to the living room, we tried our best to keep calm when both of us were actually freaking out and didn't know what to do.

"Brooke? Can you remember me?" James sat by her and asked.

I didn't know what happened but the look in her eyes had changed. They didn't look strange to me. They were her beautiful brown eye.

"Yeah! Of course, I do. I'm sorry, I should have told you about it," she said.

"About what?" I asked and sat down.

"After my accident last winter, ever since I got out of the coma, sometimes when I have a nightmare, I might not remember a thing for a while after I wake up," she said as she was looking at her hands sitting on her lap.

"Why didn't you tell me that?" James asked.

He was truly worried. She was like a little sister to him and I would feel the same if something slightly like this happened to Charlotte. I was worried about Brooke too, but not like James. He is a real big brother.

"I don't know. It hasn't happened to me for a while now so I thought it might have been gone. I'm so sorry guys," she said.

"We were just worried about you," I said.

My voice barely came out. I felt like I was choking.

"Okay! Now get some sleep," James said.

"Actually, can you still take me home Charles?" she asked.

"Yeah, sure. Just let me change," I said.

She just smiled. I went to my room to change. I wore a pair of black jeans and a black hoodie. I grabbed my jacket and keys and went back to the living room. She said goodbye to James and grabbed her stuff.

"I'm so sorry. I must have freaked you out," she said after a few minutes of silence.

"It's all right. I just got worried. I didn't know about your accident. I mean James never mentioned it," I said.

"He didn't know either," she said.

"Oh!" Was the only thing I could say.

It wasn't a big surprise. They haven't seen each other in like two years. They had a lot of catching up to do. I hoped I didn't get in the way of them talking.

"Thanks for driving me home," she said as we arrived at her place.

"No problem," I said with a smile.

She was about to leave but then she stopped and turned around.

"Will you come to my exhibition tomorrow night?" she asked.

"I always come!" I said with a smile.

Her eyes widened. She pointed at me in surprise.

"I knew I knew you from somewhere. You're the one who always buys the number ones!" she said in surprise.

She really remembered me? I couldn't believe it. I had never said my name. I bought them anonymously. But she remembered me.

"Yes!" I said with a huge smile which I couldn't help.

"Why didn't you say anything? Do you know how much I looked for you? I didn't have any name or anything else!" she said.

I just laughed.

"Oh my God! I have so many questions for you! But I really need to go," she said.

"Okay," I said.

"But we have to talk!" she said with a huge smile.

My smile got bigger and bigger. She gave me a hug, said goodbye and left. I waited until she went inside and then went home. I was pretty tired so I just went straight to bed. I needed to get some proper sleep before tomorrow. I needed to do a few other things for the selling contract and check on a few things for Sunday's concert. We really needed to do it perfectly for everyone's sake, for everyone's career.

Chapter Four

When I walked into the gallery, I was still half asleep. Even though I was drinking coffee, it was hard to keep my eyes open. The paintings were almost hung up. There were just a few left to hang. Bella was there and looking after everything. She was a real help.

"Hey boss," she said as she saw me.

"How is everything going?" I asked with a low voice.

"Everything is going great. How was the meeting last night?" she asked as she hung the last painting.

"Well, they bought the whole collection," I said.

Her jaw dropped right away. She was looking at me with wide eyes. She couldn't even say a word. I checked on everything for the last time. Someone from The Young's brought the selling contract and a check so we could wrap it up. I was going to give the check directly to the charity I was raising money for so I didn't give the check to Bella as always.

Everything was done in the gallery so I headed out to get lunch and then get ready for tonight. I was going to one of my favorite places but it was closed. So, I decided to go home and order something. But as I was walking home, I remembered that I left my scarf in the gallery so went back there to get it since it was freezing cold. I went to the back room to get my scarf but when I heard something, I froze.

"Oh, I love you, Bella," Nick said.

I knew it was him. It was his husky voice. It was the same person who accused me of cheating last night. I couldn't believe it. I took my phone out and recorded their voice. They were kissing for a while and all I could hear was moaning which disgusted me.

"I can't believe I had to share you with that bitch for the last few months," she said disgusted.

"Well, that bitch has made us two million dollars so can you be a little nicer to her? It's the last day," he said and kissed her again.

I was about to scream any minute so I put my hand on my lips to prevent any noise.

"Well, maybe just for you," she said and kissed him again.

I couldn't stand it anymore. I just left the gallery. I took a few deep breaths to calm my nerves. I didn't know what to do. I took a cab home. I couldn't stand there. They could see me. They had just confessed to robbing me. I needed to go to the police. But I didn't know if that was enough so I called the only one I thought I could call right now. I called James. He picked up after a few rings.

"James! I need your help. I just found out my assistant and my dear boyfriend have been robbing me all this time," I said as he picked up.

"Wait a minute, hold on. They robbed you?" he asked.

"Yes!" I said with anger.

"Why didn't you call your dad? He definitely knows better than me what you should do," he said carefully since he knew I didn't have a close relationship with my dad.

"No, James! You know my dad is not an option. I rather get robbed and lose two million dollars than call him!" I said.

"What's going on?" I could hear Charles from a distance.

"Brooke got robbed by her assistant and her boyfriend."
He told Charles.

"Does she have any proof?" Charles asked.

"Yeah! I could record their voice," I said and James told
Charles.

Charles was quiet for a few seconds. James put his phone
on speaker so we could talk easier.

"Where are you?" James asked.

"I'm going home," I said.

"Brooke, can you come to the office?" Charles asked.

"I don't know if I can. I need to get ready for tonight," I
said.

"Okay! Let me make a few calls. I'll call you as soon as I
can," Charles said.

"Okay. Thank you!" I said and hung up.

A few minutes later I was in my apartment. Before
anything I ordered lunch. As I was waiting for my lunch to
arrive, I grabbed a trash bag and threw every single thing that
son of a bitch left in my apartment. It wasn't much but still
there were somethings I knew he loved. I tossed them in the
trash bag and threw it out.

As my lunch arrived, I ate and then took a quick shower.
Since I didn't have much time, I didn't bother to wash my hair.
It was still clean from yesterday. I was planning to wear a short
dress but the temperature dropped in the last few days so I
deiced to wear a red suit. I matched it with a black laced
bodysuit and a pair of black high heels. I let my long hair fall
down on my back. I wore a pair of silver earrings, a black and
silver watch and two rings on each hand. I put on a full glam
makeup with a deep red velvet lipstick.

The exhibition wouldn't start for another three hours. I

didn't know what to do. Charles hasn't called me yet and I didn't know what to do about it. All I could think about to do was to check my bank account. I grabbed my laptop and checked every transaction from the last four months. I didn't even know how they did it but there were transactions to Bella's account I didn't do. I printed them and highlighted each transaction. I thought I had enough proof to get them so I called James since I didn't have Charles' number but Charles picked up.

"I've got proof!" I said as he picked up.

"Perfect. I was about to call you. I talked to my legal team. They said if you have the proof and their confession and go to the police, they can get them arrested in a few hours," Charles said.

"Thanks. But don't I need a lawyer?" I asked.

"If you had one, you could stay out of the messiness of this whole thing" Charles said.

"The problem is I don't have one!" I said.

"It's okay. I'll hook you up with my best lawyer. I'm going to the office. Can you meet me there?" he asked.

"Yeah! I'll be there in twenty minutes," I said.

I grabbed the prints and put them in a folder. I wore a long white overcoat and grabbed my purse. I was out of my apartment in no time. Fortunately, the gallery was downtown, not far from The Young's office. As I was on my way, I got a message from Charles, to go to fifth floor. When I got there, his assistant led me to his office. He was sitting there with an older man.

"Hi. Brooke, this is Mister Smith, he's our best lawyer," he said.

"Nice to meet you," I said and shook hands with him.

I told him what happened and I played them the recorded audio. They both kind of grossed out because of all the moaning in the recording. Mister Smith checked out my bank account activity and said it might be enough. Mister Smith and I went to a police station and filled a report. And since he had a very good friend there, he promised me they would get them tonight.

It would make a scene in the middle of my exhibition but I didn't mind it. There were journalists there who might write about this but again, I didn't mind. I was never afraid to be the talk of the town. Since I was a child, I had been the talk of the town every once in a while. But if it did get out, it would just show everyone that nobody messes with Brooke Edwards. Even though I heard it accidently, no one needed to know.

"How did it go?" Charles asked as I walked out of the station.

"They promised us they would arrest them tonight," I said with a little smile.

"Oh, wow! How are you feeling?" he asked.

"Well, I'll be fine when they're behind bars," I said honestly.

My exhibition would start in less than an hour. I thought we were driving to the gallery but Charles was going to their office.

"Why are you going back to your office?" I asked.

"I want to change," he said with a smile.

He already looked amazing. I didn't know why he needed to change. He was wearing a navy-blue suit with a baby blue shirt and a purple tie. He looked like a happy guy. I didn't say another word. As we got there, we went back to his office. He grabbed his suit from his closet and went to his bathroom to change. I just stood there and looked at the beautiful view of New York in the winter. It wasn't raining or snowing but it was still magical.

"Ready to go?" Charles asked and pulled me out of my thoughts.

As I turned around and saw him, I got amazed. He was looking hotter than ever. He has changed into a black suit, a white freshly ironed shirt and a deep red tie, the same color as my lipstick. I was speechless. He smiled and walked to me and stood like five inches away from me. His tie was a little crooked. My hands went to his tie to fix it subconsciously. The smile on his face got bigger.

"How do I look?" he asked like a teenage girl.

"Perfect! I think we should go," I said with a smile.

He nodded and we headed out. In less than ten minutes, we were there. We went in through the back doors to avoid the crowd in the front. As we walked into the main area, we saw Nick and Bella. Fortunately, they were not making out and our plan stayed safe.

"I thought you'd come sooner." Nick said trying to sound like a real boyfriend.

"I needed to take care of something," I said with a smirk.

"And who is the lucky guy?" he said but there was nothing in his voice.

"Charles Young," Charles said before I could say anything.

Charles put out his hand and Nick shook it. He was acting so professional. Bella didn't say a word but her jaw dropped on the ground as Charles introduced himself. Charles and I left our overcoats in the back room and went back. We all walked around the gallery for the last time and checked everything. I was keeping my eyes on them both. They were not acting like always. They were too calm and careless. There were sold signs added to the bottom of each painting.

As the clock struck six, the doors opened and people came in one by one. The gallery was soon filled with people. James arrived a little after six. I kept one eye on Bella and Nick and the other on the door. People came and went. I spent my night talking to people, journalist and bloggers. I was expecting the police to come any minute.

Mister Smith stayed at the station to make sure they'd get arrested tonight. James and Charles were drinking and watching those bastards. It was about eight when Mister Smith called me so I went somewhere less crowded to answer my phone.

"Hello?" I shouted over the crowd's noise.

"Miss Edwards? I got some news. You might want to sit down for it," he said.

"What is it?" I shouted again.

"They both have criminal records. They had robbed a few others just like they robbed you. They're both wanted. The police have got the warrant. They are on their way," he said.

"Well, that's amazing news! Thank you," I said.

I grabbed a glass of wine and went to James and Charles. The sound of police cars was getting closer and closer. I couldn't wait to see them get arrested.

"Guys, we're about to see something good!" I said with smirk and took a sip from my glass.

"Oh, and they both have criminal records. They are both wanted," I said and took another sip.

"Guys, can one of you record this?" I said with an evil smirk.

As the officers came in, I walked to them and led them to those bastards. They were looking at me with shock. They thought they had done it perfectly this time, too but they screwed it up at the last minute. I watched them getting arrested. Every journalist was taking videos or photos of what was happening so I decided to give them a little something to talk about. As the officers were taking them out, I walked in front of them to say something.

"You choose the wrong person to mess with," I said with a smirk as the room was dead silent.

I took a sip and walked away and they took them. The gallery was quiet for a few minutes but then everyone started to talk. I joined James and Charles who were still in shock.

"What the hell was that?" James asked as he was laughing.

"If I learned only one thing from growing up in the public eye, is that you can turn a story around with just a few words," I said with a smile.

"You should have studied drama not collaborative arts," James said.

"I don't need to study drama," I said with a smirk.

Charles was still in shock.

The time of the gallery was ending and people went home one by one. James met someone and invited her for a drink. Soon the gallery was empty and there was just Charles and I left. Even the team from their company had picked up the collection from the gallery. I was sitting on the ground and Charles came and sat by my side as soon as his team left.

"So, now that they are arrested, what do want to do?" he asked.

"I just want to go home, kick off my shoes because they

are killing me and order a pizza! What do you want to do?" I asked.

"I don't know," he said.

"Well, you can join me if you want to. I still have a ton of questions to ask you," I said with a smile.

"Only if you show me your studio!" he said with a smirk.

"Deal." I held out my hand and said.

He shook my hand and got up. He held out his hand. As I put my hand in his, he pulled me up. I lost my balance and almost fell on him. We grabbed our stuff, locked up and left.

Chapter Five

"Come on in!" I said as I opened the door.

As we walked in, I turned on the lights. I took off my overcoat and left it on the couch. Charles came in and took off his overcoat. I went to the kitchen to grab some beer.

"Thanks. Can I just say you look stunning," he said as I handed him the beer.

"Thanks!" I said as I blushed.

My apartment was pretty hot since I hated the cold outside. After I took off my coat, I took a few sips of my beer. Charles was looking around and didn't notice I took off my coat until he turned around to ask me about my piano.

"Do you still play?" he asked as he turned around.

As he saw me, his lips parted for a few short seconds but then he pulled himself back together. My body suit was pretty revealing, except for my breasts. He could easily see my body.

"Not really. My dad sent me the piano as a gift when I bought the apartment. It hasn't been touched," I said.

"Wow! Could you be any more successful? Eighteen and you already have everything," he said with a smile.

"Well, I don't know!" I said with a smirk.

"Can I see your studio now?" he asked.

"Yeah, just please be careful in there. You don't want to ruin your suit," I said.

He just laughed and nodded. He was wearing a French

suit which I was pretty sure was handmade. He left his coat in the living room and followed me to my studio. Since I was living in a two-bedroom apartment, I turned my second room into a painting studio.

"How did you know I work in my apartment?" I asked.

"I have a few sources," he said with a smirk.

"But really, how did you know?" I asked because I really wanted to know.

"In your last exhibition, you were talking to a journalist about where you paint and I was passing by and heard it," he said.

I couldn't believe he gave it up this easily. Yes, I did talk about my studio with a few journalists but none of them found it interesting enough to let it be published.

I left him alone in the room to go take off my makeup. As I came back, I sat on a clean stool and watched Charles going through everything. I was getting so hungry so I grabbed my phone to order some pizza. I was thinking peperoni but I didn't know if Charles like spicy food or not.

"I want to order some pizza. What do you like?" I asked.

"Peperoni." He simply said as he was going through my sketches.

I couldn't help my laugher. Did he just say that to let me know he knows exactly what I like? He looked up at me with a smile. So, yes. He was doing that.

"Did you just say peperoni because you know I like it or you actually like it?" I asked.

"Can't it be both?" he asked in return.

I just laughed a little and ordered dinner. Our beers were half way gone by this point. We both had a few drinks back in the gallery. I knew I shouldn't drink much especially that fast.

I didn't want to get drunk soon. It was only past eleven. I knew it would be a long night. I had so many questions to ask. Charles already knew everything about me and my past. He just didn't know about my accident but he even figured it out last night.

We spent some quiet time in my studio. Finally, the pizza guy pulled us out of the room. Charles wanted to pay but I didn't let him. I paid him and before you judge me to open the door with that look, I put on my jacket before opening the door. But as soon as the door was closed, I took it off again. I grabbed a couple of more beers from the fridge and went to the living room. I kicked my heels off before starting to eat.

"So, tell me, why you came to my first gallery?" I asked before taking a bite.

"Okay, I heard about it from one of my best art consultants that you're putting together an exhibition and she was like 'Oh, another rich kid thinks that she's an artist'. But I remembered your name from James' stories so I came without telling anyone," he said, and took a bite.

"Okay fair enough. Most of the people who came to my first exhibition thought the same way. What does she think about my work now?" I asked.

"Let's just say she tried to deny what she said," he said and laughed.

I laughed with him. I didn't blame anyone who thought this way at first. I wasn't the first rich kid who thought they were an artist and put on an exhibition. The difference is that I'm actually an artist.

"Wait. You said your art consultant? I thought the company was your father's!" I said after a few seconds.

"No. It's actually mine. Most of it at last," he said.

"Why do you have so many pieces of me? What do you do with it?" I asked and took another bite.

"You really don't know?" he asked and I just shook my head no in return.

"Well, we are actually an art dealing company. We collect the best pieces from all over the world for art collectors," he said.

"Wow. How did you even get into such thing?" I asked.

"Well, since I was fifteen or sixteen, I was going to different exhibitions with my dad. He always loved art and had been a collector for years. So naturally I started to think about a way to make this easier for art collectors to find pieces they want to buy. So, I gathered the best art consultants in New York and founded The Young's Arts with the help of my dad," he said.

"I wished my parents cared that much!" I said and sighed.

I took a big bite from my pizza to keep myself from talking. I knew if I talked about it, I'd cry.

"Why would you say that?" he asked and loosened his tie a little.

"Haven't you notice that neither of my parents have come to my exhibitions?" I asked.

"I noticed but don't you know your dad has a few pieces of yours?" he asked confused.

"How'd you know that?" I asked.

"Isn't your dad Logan Edwards?" he asked and I nodded.

"I know for a fact that he has just three pieces of your last collection," he said.

What? Was it true? I didn't know. I just felt like choking. I took a few sips from my beer to get rid of the choking. Tears were forming in my eyes. I was blinking fast to get rid of them.

"Why do you always pick my number ones?" I asked to change the subject.

"In all of your galleries, your number ones were always the best ones," he said with a little smile.

I think he could see I wasn't feeling good. I needed to get my mind away from my dad as much as possible.

"Did you know the number one from your first gallery is now worth about a million dollars?" he asked after a few minutes of silence.

What? It was about five times the price I sold it for. Was it actually real? I knew my pieces were going to be worth more after a few collections but I didn't know it would happen this fast. I had my first exhibition in August and now four months later it's worth five times its original price. I was kind of glad. It showed I was growing as an artist. But wasn't I growing too fast? I was scared of getting back in the spotlight. I needed a break from the light for some time. That was why I started to paint at the first place. I wanted to stay away from everything but instead I pushed myself back into the lights even more than before.

"Wow! That's amazing," I said happily and took a sip.

"I thought the anonymous guy would come back and buy his third number one," I said.

"Oh, I'm going to keep the number one for myself," he said with a smirk.

"I hope I can keep your collection of number ones gorgeous," I said and took a sip.

"I hope you will," he said.

I noticed his beer was empty so I got up to take another one for him. I was good. I knew by the end of the bottle I was drinking; I would be drunk. He thanked me as I handed him the bottle.

"So, when should I expect your next exhibition?" he asked.

It just made me laugh. It hasn't been even a day since I wrapped up my last exhibition and he wants to know when's the next one. But he didn't know I was actually thinking about taking a break or work a little slower.

"Actually, I don't know. I might take a break or work a little slower," I said.

"Why?" he asked with wide eyes.

"Because I'm always working. I don't have much time for myself and my projects for school are just getting harder and harder. I just don't want to get sick of it," I said.

"Yeah! That makes a lot of sense," he said.

"So, James told you a lot about me. What exactly he told you?" I asked.

I was actually scared of what he could've told Charles about me. I was a troublemaker in school. James and Ben would always get me out of trouble but as they graduated, my troublemaking days graduated with them!

"He told me about the parties you and your brother threw. He told me about the time you blew up your chemistry class; the time you put black coloring in the boy's showering system; and the time you 'accidentally' burnt you teacher's hair and eyebrows; and I think every single thing you did!" he said with laughter.

I was so embarrassed that I couldn't look at him. I turned red. I think I did worse than these things. I couldn't quite remember.

"I always wondered why you did all these things to guys. You never did anything to girls?" He asked.

"Because I'm a girl!" I said with laughter.

He laughed with me. The pizza box was empty. The bottles were empty and the coffee table had turned into a recycle table. So, I got up to clean it up. But as I got up to take them to the kitchen, I felt a heavy dizziness in my head and fell on the couch, near Charles.

"Are you okay?" he asked but couldn't hold back his laughter.

I nodded as I was laughing. It's been so long since I've been this drunk and happy. I looked at him as he was still laughing. His hair was mostly in his face driving my attention to his beautiful green eyes which was now a little darker and looked more gray than green. He brushed a little piece of my hair out of my face and put it behind my ear.

He slipped his hand to my bare neck and shoulder. My skin was burning under his touch. He played with the strap of my body suit a little. His hand slid back to my neck and then into my hair. I was still and completely silent the entire time. My eyes closed subconsciously under his touch. I had no idea what was happening. I had no idea what he was going to do. I just wanted to get burnt. He pulled a little closed but then stopped.

I opened my eyes and stared into his. They were red and wild. He looked at my lips and then into my eyes. He didn't say a thing. I didn't neither. He just pulled me in swiftly and kissed me slowly. I kissed him back. I put a hand on the back of his neck and a hand on his shoulder. He put his other hand on my waist and kept me close but not too close. His lips were soft and bitter from the beer. He kept kissing me slowly and steady for a few minutes. I was going out of breath when he moved on to my lower neck.

He was kissing me so gently that if he'd kissed my neck for a whole day, it wouldn't leave a mark. I ran my fingers through his hair and kept his head on my neck. I threw back my head a little in pleasure. My breaths came out more unsteady each second that he kept kissing my neck. His hand moved from my waist to my back and pulled me a little closer.

I was getting hotter and hotter each second. I pulled away a little. He got confused. But then I put my hands on his shoulders and pulled myself a little up. I slipped one knee to his other side and sat on his lap. I slipped my hands to his neck and pulled him closed. He slipped his hands to my waist slowly and pulled me as close as he could. He kissed my lips and I kissed him back.

I didn't know where we would end up tonight but I didn't actually care. Not that I didn't care about his feeling but we both knew we wanted it. I didn't know if we would hook up or not. I didn't know if I was ready or not. I just knew I wanted to enjoy his lips.

I slipped my hands to his collar and unbuttoned a few buttons of his shirt. I slipped my hands into his hair and pulled his head a little back. I moved on to his check, his earlobe and his neck. I knew I didn't want to get too wild with him. He was so gentle and I was enjoying it. He was nothing like that son of a bitch.

Charles let out a sigh in pleasure. I smiled on his neck and kissed his Adams apple and moved on to the other side. He put his hands on my face and pulled me up from his neck. He just kept staring into my eyes for a few seconds in complete silence. His eyes were back to green again. He was about to kiss me again when his phone rang and pulled us apart. I got up from his lap.

As he saw James' name on the screen, he picked up. We didn't notice how time had flown. It was around two in the morning.

"Hi…! Yeah. We got caught up in something… I don't know. I probably take a cab," he said on the phone.

"Why don't you stay?" I said and hoped he'd spend the night.

"Or I might stay… okay. Don't wait up. Bye," he said and hung up.

He left his phone on the coffee table. He wrapped his arm around my shoulder and pulled my close. I rested my head on his shoulder.

"You'll stay?" I asked.

"If you let me," he said.

I laughed a little and kissed him on the lips. I rested my head back on his shoulder. We both were pretty tired and drunk. I closed my eyes for a few seconds but then I fell asleep.

I woke up in the middle of the night with the sound of rain and lightnings. I was on top of Charles, laying on the couch. He was asleep. He looked so gorgeous. I just put my head back on his chest and fell asleep again.

Chapter Six

I woke up pretty early. It was a couple of minutes before seven. Charles was soundly asleep. I watched him for a while but then got up and covered him with a blanket. I threw the empty pizza box and the bottles in the recycle can. I took a quick shower and dried my hair and let it fall on my back. I knew I wasn't going anywhere important today so didn't bother to straighten it.

As I went back to the living room Charles was still asleep. I smiled subconsciously at the way his hair shone under the dim light coming from the window. I could tell he was blond when he was a kid but now his hair is a very light shade of brown. I couldn't get enough of him but I had to. I was starving. I went to kitchen to decide what to do for breakfast. I had mostly everything except for orange juice and milk.

I wore something comfortable and warm to go to the grocery store. It was close so I didn't have to take a cab or anything. It was only a block away. I left a note for Charles so if he'd wake up, he wouldn't freak out.

As I was walking to the grocery store, I thought about last night and what happened between the two of us. I couldn't deny I was attracted to him from the day I bumped into him in the hallway. He was pretty handsome and a total gentleman. Nobody could deny it. But what happened last night, was it just a drunk move or was he actually into me? I really wanted to know. And here's the important part, I didn't have any bad dreams or nightmares. I haven't had a sleep like this in months! I always have nightmares.

When I got home, Charles was still asleep. I put the groceries on the island and changed into a pair of canary yellow yoga pants and a black and white T-shirt. I wanted to make some pancakes. I was half way done when Charles woke up. I think the smell of the pancakes woke him up.

"Wow! Pancakes?" he asked with his eye half way closed.

"Yeah! How'd you sleep?" I asked because I slept amazing last night.

"Surprisingly good. Your couch is pretty comfortable! How'd you sleep?" he asked.

"Pretty good actually. I haven't had a good sleep like that in months," I said honestly.

The smile on his face doubled. He went to the bathroom to wash up and I finished the pancakes. I put them on two plates and put a couple of strawberries and slices of banana on them. I wasn't sure he like syrup or Nutella on his pancakes so I just left them on the island.

"Oh my God! I'll come here every morning for breakfast," he said with his mouth full of pancakes.

I just laughed and didn't say anything. We hardly said a single word during breakfast. We just ate. As we finished, he helped me with the dishes and cleaning the kitchen.

"Brooke? Can we talk?" he asked seriously.

I was a hundred percent sure he wanted to talk about last night but I didn't know if it was a good talk or a bad talk. I took a deep breath and hoped for the best.

"Sure!" I said with a little smile.

"I was going to wait a while but after what happened last

night, I don't think I have to anymore. Umm, can I take you to dinner some time?" he asked like a gentleman.

I couldn't help my smile or the way I blushed. It was so sweet of him. I never thought he would be this thoughtful. I walked up to him, got on the tip of my toes and kissed him.

"Sure," I said with a huge smile on my face.

The smile on his lips couldn't get any bigger. He grabbed me by my waist and lifted me up a little and kissed me. As we were kissing his phone rang again and, just like last night, it was James.

"Dude, your timing is the worst… oh, shit! I totally forgot about the rehearsals… Okay, okay. I'm coming," he said and hung up.

"Apparently we have rehearsals this morning," he said with laughter as he wore his shoes.

I just laughed. He was out of my apartment in five minutes. He kissed me before he left. I didn't have anything to do so I just decided to clean up a little and watch some TV. But before I could start, Mister Smith called me to meet him at the station as soon as possible.

I got ready and went to the police station. They give them a lawyer because they didn't have one themselves. I didn't want to see their faces so I let Mister Smith handle as much as he could. We wouldn't go to court more than once since there was too many evidences. But since it was Saturday, we couldn't do much. I just had to go there to confirm who they were.

I was going back to my place when Charles called me. I was shocked he called me. He had rehearsals. It must have been something important that he called.

"Hi. How are you?" I said as I picked.

"Hi. Not good! I need to ask you a favor," he said and waited for my response.

"Sure. What is it?" I asked.

Honestly after helping me out yesterday, I really owed him a lot. I really don't know what would've happened if he didn't help me out yesterday.

"One of our pianists got food poisoning. Can you play with us tomorrow night?" he asked.

"Sure. But I can't promise to be perfect. I haven't touched a piano in months," I said.

"It's okay. Just come here. We'll figure it out," he said.

"Okay. Just send me the location," I said.

"Okay," he said.

They were at one of Tisch's theaters. It was close to my apartment so I just told the cab driver to take me there. Fifteen minutes later I was there. There were about thirty people on the stage and on the seats, waiting for a miracle. As I got close to the stage, Charles and James noticed me. I gave both of them a hug. They introduced me to everyone. I watched a couple of jaws dropping as they introduced me.

None of them could rehearse without me knowing the pieces completely so they left. There was no point in staying anyway.

"So, what am I playing?" I asked.

"Here. These are the pieces we're going to play." Charles handed a bunch of sheet music.

I went through them one by one. They were mostly the pieces I had played before. I was just worried because I haven't played a note in almost a year. The last time I sat on a piano and played anything was last Christmas when Ben came home and I played a few of our favorite songs.

"I used to play most of these songs. But I'm not sure if I still can remember how to play them," I said.

"It's okay! Give it a try," James said.

I nodded and sat on the piano. Then I noticed there's another piano on the other side of the stage. I didn't know why it was even there. It was unusual. Charles said on the phone they lost a pianist. I really didn't think about it till now! Charles and James sat down and I started to play. I couldn't believe I still could play those songs. A few took me a couple of tries to figure out. James left to get lunch after a few pieces I played.

As I got up from the piano, Charles ran on the stage, hugged me, lifted me up and spun me around. I wrapped my arms around his neck for support. He kissed me as he put me down on the stage.

"How was it?" I asked as he pulled away.

"Perfect," he said with a huge smile.

I just smiled with all of my heart. I felt more appreciated than ever. He really knew how to treat a woman.

"Why there's another piano on the stage?" I asked.

"I'm playing it," he said.

"Two pianos at the same time?" I asked.

"Technically we'll play different things," he said.

"What do you mean?" I asked.

"Let me show you," he said

He gave me the sheet music for the performance. We were actually performing one piece but each of us would play different parts from the other. We played a piece with the performance sheet music. It wasn't as hard as I thought it would be but we needed to work on them. When James came back, we let it go and ate lunch on the stage.

"So, how is she?" James asked Charles.

He knew for a fact that if he asked me, I would say I was awful. He has seen me do that a lot.

"She's pretty good actually. I think we can get it right by tonight," Charles said.

But I wasn't sure. I mean if I was playing alone, I'd be all right but when we're going to play this way, I didn't even know if we could get it right by tomorrow night.

"I really don't know," I said hopelessly.

"Please don't! You always see the worst thing that could happen when it's not even possible," James said.

"I agree. You were pretty good. I'm sure you'll blow their minds away tomorrow," Charles said.

"I hope so," I said.

"I'm sure you will," Charles said and took my hand in his and kissed it.

James was looking at us with the most confused and curious look ever. He had no idea what happened last night or what didn't happen!

"Is there anything I need to know?" he asked.

I just blushed and looked down. Charles didn't say a thing either. Our silence and my blushing told James everything and even maybe more than what actually happened.

"You're kidding me!" he said in shock.

"I just asked her out!" Charles said and kept it simple.

"You just asked her out and she's practically turned into a tomato?" James asked like he didn't believe Charles.

"And a little more than that," I said.

"Oh my God! As much as I am happy for both of you, but I have to say you're crazy!" James said.

"Yeah! But we're the good kind of crazy," I said with a

smirk while looking at Charles.

James didn't say anything else. We finished our lunch and went back to rehearsing. We played and played and played. My fingers were sore but I didn't say a thing. I knew if they knew, they wouldn't let me play anymore. So, I kept my face straight and played.

I was getting pretty tired. But I wanted to get them right. We stayed there till nine. By the time we left the theater Charles and I were so tired that we could barely move. James texted everyone that we'll have the final rehearsals and the sound check at noon tomorrow.

We went back to their apartment to relax and rest a little. I didn't even know if I would be able to go home tonight. I just wanted to lay down and do nothing. We didn't do much. We were pretty tired so we ate dinner and just watched a little TV.

I fell asleep on the couch for a few minutes but Charles woke me up so I could get changed and sleep on his bed. My clothes were not comfortable to sleep in so I borrowed a pair sweatpants and a T-shirt from Charles and changed.

"They look better on you," he said as I came out of his bathroom.

"Sure!" I said and laughed weakly.

I got under the covers and he wrapped his arms around me and I rested my head on his chest.

"Thank you for today," he said as he was playing with my hair.

"Don't even mention it. It's nothing compared to what you did for me yesterday," I said.

"How much your fingers hurt?" he asked.

"What?" I asked and tried to hide the pain.

"How much your fingers hurt?" he asked again.

"They don't." I lied which I wasn't good at.

I could play pretend in front of strangers but not in front of my friends and family.

"Brooke, I can see the pain in your face! Come on. How much does it hurt?" he asked.

He held my hands in his and caressed them gently.

"Okay it hurts a little. But it's just because I haven't played in a while. That's it!" I said.

"Are you sure?" he said and I nodded.

He looked at me with a little smiled. I kissed him and he kissed me back. I put my head back on his chest and before we knew it, we both were asleep.

Chapter Seven

She put her head back on my chest and closed her eyes. She fell asleep within a minute. She was pretty tired. I couldn't actually believe how she didn't stop rehearsing till she got it perfectly right. Her fingers were so sore tonight that it was hard for her to hold her pizza. She tried to stay strong and don't show how much they hurt. I played with her hair a little till I fell asleep.

She was still asleep when I woke up. It wasn't so soon. It was around nine. I watched her for a while before getting up and taking a shower. She was still asleep when I came out of shower. I put on some comfortable clothes and went to the kitchen to make something for breakfast. When I went to the kitchen, James was already there, making breakfast.

"Good morning," I said.

"Morning! Brooke's still not awake?" he asked.

"Nope!" I said and poured myself a cup of coffee.

"I think you'd better wake her up. We should be at the theater in like two hours," he said.

"It's two hours," I said.

"Charles, It's just two hours. She needs to go back to her place and get a dress and whatever she needs for tonight," he said.

Then I realized he was right. She probably wants to take a shower and do her hair. So, I poured her a cup of coffee and went to wake her up. I was feeling like the devil by waking her up. I put the cup on the nightstand and called her with a low voice. I didn't want to scare her. She woke up fast.

"Good morning sunshine!" I said as she opened her eyes.

"Good morning!" she said as she was rubbing her eyes.

"What time is it?" she asked with her sleepy voice.

"Ten, I think," I said.

Her eyes widened and got up fast. She ran to the bathroom and came out with her clothes on and her hair tied up into a bun. She grabbed the coffee cup and drank some of it.

"I need to go home," she said.

"I'll take you." I simply said.

"You'll get stuck in the traffic. I'll take a cab," she said and took another sip.

"Okay. But first come eat something. You didn't eat much last night," I said.

She just nodded. We went to the kitchen and found the table all set up. James surprised us pretty much. She ate a little, nothing like a proper breakfast.

"Can you just pick me up later?" she asked as she got up.

"I will but you didn't even eat half of your breakfast," I said anxiously.

"I can't eat any more now," she said.

"Oh, I almost forgot. What should I wear?" she asked.

"Well, we're all gonna wear black. But it's okay if you want to wear anything else," James said.

"Okay," she said.

She gave both of us a hug and went home. We just kept eating our breakfast in silence. I was kind of worried to talk to James about Brooke but we had to.

"So, how are you two doing?" he finally asked.

"We're good. I'm trying not rush into anything too soon. I mean she broke up with him like two days ago. Even though he was a cheating son of a bitch, I don't feel right rushing into everything with her," I said delicately.

"It's good. I really don't want your relationship to get messy," he said.

"I don't either. I really like her and I'll do anything it takes to make her happy and make her feel safe," I said.

"Did you tell her your family will come tonight?" he asked.

"Shit! I totally forgot to tell her about that! Should I even tell her? Isn't it too soon for her to see them?" I asked.

I was starting to freak out. She knew my dad but meeting him and my siblings as my girlfriend, wasn't it too much? I could ask her honestly and see what she says.

"I don't know. I mean she knows your dad. It's just Charlotte and Christian. But introducing your girlfriend to your family in the first two days might kind of put her under pressure!" he said.

"I think I'll just ask her," I said.

"If you're going to ask her, ask her after the performance. She's under enough pressure with the performance. I was surprised how she was working so hard yesterday," he said.

"Yeah! I can't distract her," I said.

I didn't tell him about our talk last night. She was in pain but she didn't want us to know. My head was spinning around this whole thing the whole time I was getting ready. I picked out the perfect black suite, a freshly ironed white shirt and a black tie. I completed my outfit with a pair of black leather shoes and a matching belt. I needed to look perfect for two reasons.

The first one was Brooke. She might not study fashion but she's always wearing the best outfits. She really brings out the suiting up side of me. And the second reason was all the journalists we've invited. We were hoping to get some recognition. So many of us needed it. I really didn't know what I wanted to do after collage so I needed to keep my options available, including music.

As we got ready, I called to check on Brooke. She was ready. We picked her up and went to the theater. She was still pretty stressed out. We had a rehearsal and a quick sound check to make sure our instruments sounded perfect. James was leading the orchestra. Besides Brooke, James was the most stressed out person there. Most of them was so relaxed and chilled.

As we did the rehearsals, I watched everyone's jaw drops. I could say everybody knew Brooke. She was pretty famous and ever since she started to work as a painter, she became even more famous. So many people adored her and admired her work.

She was the rich girl who left home in everyone's eyes. She couldn't stay out of the lights. She was born in the lights and she grew in the lights. And as I'm seeing her now, she will always stay in the lights.

It was getting closer and closer to the performance. In less than an hour we would be performing. I haven't asked her about meeting my family yet. I still didn't know if I should even ask her or not. We haven't even been on a date yet.

The girls were getting ready in their dressing rooms. And I was just pacing back and forth on the stage. I was getting nervous. Not for the performance but about talking to Brooke. Girls came out of the rooms one by one. I could hear the crowd getting louder and louder. Brooke was the last one to walk out of her room.

She looked like a goddess. She was wearing a simple makeup but her lipstick was deep red, my favorite. She was wearing a long black silk dress. It was pretty revealing. The neckline was so low that her breasts were showing a little. The back was low, too but her long straight hair was pretty much covering it. She was wearing a pair of classic black high heels. I didn't even know how she could play with those heels but then if she couldn't, she wouldn't wear them!

"Wow! You look breathtaking!" I said after a few minutes.

"Thank you! You look pretty nice, too," she said with a smile.

We walked to the stage together and sat at the pianos. The curtains were still closed. They would open up any minute now. I took a few deep breaths and got ready. If I missed even a note, I would ruin it for everyone. I was a little worried about Brooke, too. She didn't eat even a bite since this morning. I tried to convince her to eat lunch but she said she was too stressed out to eat anything. She just drank some water. Unfortunately, I was just like her. I can't eat when I'm stressed out.

As the curtains opened up, I pushed my stress away and tried my best to give a perfect performance. One and a half hours went by pretty fast. But fortunately, it went by well. Brooke was pretty confident behind the piano. I thought she played even better than I did. I would look up at her to make sure she was all right every once in a while, but not for long. Because if I did, I might have just screwed up.

As the performance ended and the curtains closed, I ran to her and hugged her, lifted her up and spun her around on the stage. She wrapped her arms around my neck as soon as I picked her up. I kissed her red lips before putting her down.

"You were amazing!" I said as she was still in my arms.

"I had a good leader," she said with a smile and kissed me again.

"Oh God! Get a room!" James said after she broke off the kiss.

I put her down and she pulled away to go give him a hug too. As we were alone on the stage, I took her hand and we sat on the piano's bench. I was still not sure if I should even ask her but I did anyway.

"So, my family's here if you like to meet them," I said.

"When you say family, who should I expect except from your dad?" she asked.

"My little sister and my twin brother," I said.

"You have a twin?" she asked with wide eyes.

"Yeah!" I said.

"So, what do you think? Do you want to meet them? I mean no pressure. I just wanted to let you know they are here if you'd liked to meet them. But really, it's no big deal if you don't want…," I was saying but she stopped me.

She put a finger on my lips and shushed me.

"I'd love to meet your family," she said with a smile.

She took her finger off of my lips and then put a little kiss on my lips. The smile on my lips couldn't get any bigger. I took her hand and dragged her to where they were sitting. My dad was smiling at us with the biggest smile ever.

"Hi, thanks for coming," I said and gave everyone a hug.

"Guys, this is the one and only Brooke Edwards, our life saver and my girlfriend," I introduced her to everyone.

"Nice to meet you!" she said and shook hands with

everyone.

Charlotte spent more than ten minutes admiring Brooke's dress. Christian teased me as much as he could and well my dad was being my dad and just said 'I told you!'.

After they left, we went back to our dressing rooms and changed into out warm and more comfortable clothes. Brooke even took off her makeup. As we got out of the theater, it was past eight. We went straight to our place. As we got home, James put his stuff in his room and changed.

"Goodbye kids! Don't wait up," he said as he was leaving.

He didn't even wait to get questioned where he was heading to. He was either going to a bar and hitting on some girls or he was seeing a girl and didn't want to tell us.

"So, what should we do?" I asked.

"I say we put on some comfortable clothes on, order food and watch a movie," she said.

So, we did as she suggested. She wore the clothes I gave her last night. Before I ordered diner, I turned up the heat. It was getting colder and colder every day in New York and I really wasn't the biggest fan of this freezing cold. I liked rainy and snowy days but a cold day without rain or snow was not my favorite day.

As we both were pretty tired and cold, we decided to watch the movie in my bedroom under a warm blanket. We ordered pizza so it would be easier to eat in bed. We put on Knives Out and got under the blanket. I preferred not to watch a romantic movie tonight. It could lead us both where we would regret tomorrow morning. Well, I wouldn't but she might.

Our pizza arrived after a while. We ate as we watched the movie. Brooke tried her best to stay awake till the end of the movie but she fell asleep near the end so I just turned the TV off so it wouldn't wake her up. I covered her up as she was in my arms. I watched her for a while but then I tuned off the lights and just slept.

Chapter Eight

I woke up in his arms. My head was still buried in his chest. I looked up at him. He was still asleep. His hair was falling down on his face and covering most of his beautiful forehead. I brushed it away a little to see his beautiful forehead and his closed eyes. His eyelashes were lined up perfectly. I was watching him sleep for a while before he woke up.

"Morning!" he said with a sleepy voice.

I brushed his hair out of his face and gave him a kiss.

"Good morning!" I said on his lips.

He put his hand on my waist and laid me on my back and got on me. He was kissing me gently. I ran my fingers through his slightly long hair and played with it. He placed his kisses on my lips, cheek and my neck. As I was going to pull him back up to kiss his lips, the door opened.

Charles jumped off of me like a fourteen years old guy who was caught by his girlfriend's parents. But we were interrupted by James again. He opened the door without knocking. He was covering his eyes with his hand just in case we were naked.

"Have you ever heard of something called knocking?" I asked as I sat up.

"Yeah! Can I open my eyes?" he asked.

"Just open your eyes before you embarrass both of us more than this," Charles said.

We were both fully clothed and maybe even a little too clothed. James took his hand off of his eyes. He let out a deep breath probably because we weren't naked.

"So, what was so important that you just barged in here?" I asked.

"Guys, have you checked your phones yet?" James asked.

"No! Why?" I asked.

"Let's just say your phone is about to blow up," James said with a huge smile on his face.

"Can you be more specific?" Charles said.

"Well, you two are everywhere. Everybody's talking about Brooke's exhibition and last night's performance," James said.

"That can't be right," I said trying to figure out what was happening.

"Remember your epic dramatic performance on the night of exhibition? It's trending," he said.

It was still hard for me to believe so I just grabbed my phone and turned it on. He was right. My phone was blowing up. I had at least one notification from every single website I would read news at. My social media was exploding. I muted my phone after a few seconds. I couldn't stand the sound.

I just put my phone away and tried to figure out what was actually happening. I knew for sure the story of me getting robbed would go public so I had to make sure I could shut the rumors down before they could get out of hand. But now it was getting out of hand.

I put my head on my hands, playing with my hair. I didn't know if it was a good thing or the worst thing that could happen to me. It wasn't just about me. If they wrote about last night they might have written about James and Charles as well and the rest of them. I had no idea what we needed to do.

"What are they saying?" Charles asked after a while.

He probably was worried about this whole thing. It could affect his company, too.

"They're actually saying pretty nice things about last night. And Brooke couldn't be more of a badass. Everybody's talking about *the* Edwards' power," James said.

"So, I actually didn't get the credit for standing up for myself, my dad did," I said as I lifted my head.

"Some of them want to sit with us for an interview, you can clear everything up," James said.

I couldn't say a thing. I was tired of living in my dad's shadow. I might be the girl who left her family to be on her own but I will always be Brooke Edwards, the daughter of Logan Edwards.

"Let's not judge before we read everything they said," Charles said as he took my hand in his.

"He's right. I haven't even read any of the articles either," James said.

"So, how would you know what's going on?" I asked and got up from the bed.

James couldn't look at me. He was looking around the room. I walked to him and stood a few inches away from him.

"James? How do you know what's going on?" I asked once again slowly.

"Ben called," he said as he was looking down.

"What? He called you and not me?" I said as tears was taking shape in my eyes.

"Actually, I met him last night after the concert," he said.

Suddenly I felt like my feet couldn't hold my weight any more. My knees were shaking. I couldn't stand any more. I fell, and my knees hit the ground pretty hard. It hurt a lot. Charles ran to me and tried to lift me off of the ground but I couldn't stand. He lifted me up on his arms and put me on his bed.

My tears were falling down on my cheeks. I haven't seen him for almost a year and when he came back, he didn't even bother to call me? What is he trying to prove? What have I ever done to him? James left the room and came with a glass of water. He handed me the glass and waited till I took a sip.

"Why didn't he call me? Where is he even staying?" I asked.

"I think you should talk to him about it. But he's staying at the Plaza," he said.

James left after a few minutes of silence. I still couldn't believe he was in town and didn't bother to call me or even let me know he's back. I haven't even talked to him since I got out of coma and got my memories back. Every time I tried to call him, he wouldn't answer. He wouldn't call me back. So, I just gave up. It wasn't fair. I was trying to fix everything but they were acting like I was dead so I died for them as well. I left home and didn't contact any of them again.

"Brooke?" Charles called after a while.

As I looked up at him, he pulled me in his arms and held me tight. I wrapped my arms around his waist and pulled him even closer. He kissed my head a couple of times.

"Charles, I haven't seen him in almost an entire year. I've missed him so much. And now he's back in town, he didn't even bother to call me? How can I…" I was saying but he cut me off.

He put his lips on mine and stopped me. I put my hand on his face and pulled him towards myself. I just needed to get my mind off of Ben.

"I think we should eat something first," he said after a couple of kisses.

We got up from the bed. I washed my face before going out to the kitchen. As I opened Charles' bedroom door, the smell of pancakes filled my lungs. I knew James made them. I knew exactly how his pancakes smelled like.

I sat on the table and stayed quiet. I didn't want to talk. My mind was exploding with thoughts. First the robbery then all the articles and now Ben is in town. It was too much for me to take in a short period of time. I'm used to be under pressure but I never was good at any kind of personal problems.

"Brooke? Ben wants to see you," James said half way through the breakfast.

The place was dead silent before that. The only sound you could hear was the sound of forks on the plats.

"Why didn't he just call me? I still have a phone," I said and rolled my eyes.

I was sad. I was mad. I was heartbroken. I was so hurt that I barely could feel normal. I was too afraid to get numb. Every single time I feel a little better, the world punches me in the face harder than the last time. I just wanted to get rid of all the pain and sorrow. But how could I without getting numb?

"I don't know Brooke but he's sorry. He said he's so proud of you. He said you've never sounded better," he said with a little smile.

"What? How would he know how I played with you guys last night?" I asked confused.

But then it hit me. He must've been there. There was no other explanation for it. If he wasn't there last night how the hell would he know how I performed?

"He was there last night," he said in a low voice.

I just couldn't take it anymore. I just got up and went to the balcony. I needed some fresh air. It was freezing outside but I couldn't stand there anymore. I didn't expect James to keep this from me. Especially after the night he made me promise not to keep anything from him. How could he do this to me?

James came to the balcony with a blanket after a while. He just wrapped it around my shoulders and didn't say a thing for a while.

"Why didn't you say anything sooner?" I asked.

"He didn't know if you wanted to see him or not," he said.

"Of course, I want to see him. What's he thinking?" I said as tears ran down my face again.

"When did he come to town?" I asked after a few minutes.

"A couple of days ago. He said some pretty nice things about your exhibition, too," he said.

"He came?" I asked as tears fell faster on my face.

"Yeah!" he said.

I couldn't ask another thing. I was killing myself. We stayed there a little while longer. We were freezing so we went back inside. As we went back, Charles was on the phone with someone and he sounded pretty serious.

"Okay, I'll let her know," he said and hung up.

"What's going on?" I asked.

"You have to go to court this afternoon. Are you ready for that?" he asked.

"Ready to get two million dollars back? Hell yeah!" I said.

"Good, you should be there at five," he said.

It was only eleven so I had a pretty good amount of time.

We hung out at their place for a while and checked our phones to see what they were saying about us. They were all pretty good. Some of them wanted an interview with us to get some inside information. I picked a few of the most famous and important journalists to interview with but we needed to decide this together. But we didn't have much time. Friday was Christmas and we might need to do the interviews before that.

The last thing I came across with was a video of a YouTuber. Apparently, she was making videos about what happens around New York every day. I didn't know why I was in the title of her video so I played it to find out. It wasn't long so I didn't have to wait that much. As she started to talk about me, she put a video of me in the gallery saying, 'You choose the wrong person to mess with.'

"Well as some of you may already know, that was Brooke Edwards, Logan Edwards's daughter AKA one of the most powerful men in New York. An inside source told me, her assistant and her now ex-boyfriend robbed her. But she turned the table around. She played it cool and just let them think that she had no clue. Long story short, she put two criminals in the hands of justice. So as a New Yorker, I should thank her and whomever helped her to get these criminals. Another inside source told me they were planning to run away with ten million dollars cash, the next day they got caught. I hope they get what they really deserve," she said.

I paused the video and leaned back on the couch. I was trying to decide if it was a good thing or a bad thing. As they always say there's no such thing as bad press. But I really wasn't sure about it. I mean a fake news could ruin someone like me. I really needed to pull myself back together for the court this afternoon. I had to win it and win it gloriously. With all these articles, I think I should expect a bunch paparazzi in front of the courthouse.

It was getting late. It was past two already so I wanted to go home. Charles offered to take me. He said he had to do a few things in the office before the court.

"So, what are you going to do?" he asked on the way.

"About what?" I asked since I didn't know what he was talking about.

"About Ben," he said.

"I want to see him. But I'll think about it after the court. I can't handle all of these at the same time. I just hope I won't have to go to the court more than once," I said.

"I don't think you will. Mister Smith said they confessed. The court shouldn't even take longer than half an hour," he said.

He was so calm. It made me calm down. To be honest I was freaking out myself. After the court I'll think about seeing Ben and then we can decide about the interviews. Christmas was in less than a week and I'd rather finish this whole thing before that. I just want to spend my Christmas resting at home and staying in all day long and watch every movie that had come out in the last few months.

As I got home, I kissed Charles goodbye, grabbed my last night's stuff from the back seat and went in. I didn't have much time. I put my dress and shoes in the closet and picked out something more suitable for the court. I picked out my black suit and a pair of back high heels with a dark gray long-sleeved blouse. I put on just a little makeup to cover the bags under my eyes. I didn't go too crazy with my makeup, just a simple natural make up with a nude lipstick. I wore a pair of pearl earrings and a silver watch.

I told Charles not to pick me up and meet me at the courthouse. It wasn't far from my apartment. I grabbed a black overcoat and a black purse and got out of the apartment. It was even colder than last night or the night before. I didn't know if James would come or not but if he did, it would put me in a better place. I really could use the support.

I got there a little early and as I was expecting there were photographer everywhere. As I got inside, I found Mister Smith in the hall looking a little worried.

"Thank god you are here. We need to talk," he said.

"Sure. Is everything all right?" I asked trying to keep calm.

"They want to call you to the stand; you will be under oath. You have to tell the truth," he said.

"Is there something I should know about being called?" I asked.

"Well, they might have found out that you caught them at the last minute. It wouldn't matter normally but there will be people in that room who could ruin you after what you said the night of your exhibition," he said.

"So, what can I do? I can't lie. Can't I just not answer?" I asked.

"Not answering is not an option. The only way out of it is to say simple things like you never trusted them or I don't know, you noticed money missing from your bank account," he said.

"But it is also lying. Well, somehow. I never trusted Nick but Bella was pretty convincing. What if I say all these things and they figure out I'm somehow lying?" I asked.

"So just say you never trusted him. Don't let them get under your skin. Okay?" he said.

I just nodded. I took a pill to keep my heartbeat normal. A few minutes before they called us to go to the courtroom, Charles and James arrived. Seeing them both warmed my heart. I really needed them both.

They called us and we went to the courtroom. Charles and James sat in the front row. I just wanted this to end. I felt a little sick when they brought them in. I wished the judge send them both to jail for a long time. They could face twenty-five years and more. I was feeling even sicker but as the judge came in and we all stood for him, I calmed down a little.

The court went by pretty fast until their lawyer called me to the stand. I tried my best to keep calm. Their lawyer looked even more evil than them. But as I got to the stand and sat down, I saw someone who I haven't seen in a year. Ben was there.

"Miss Edwards tell us what happened," he asked.

"Can you be more specific?" I asked politely.

"How did you find out that you've been robbed?" he asked.

"When a huge amount of money misses from your bank account, you check every transition," I said.

"So, you knew all along?" he asked with an evil smirk.

I knew what he was doing. He was trying to get under my skin. But I couldn't let that happen.

"Somehow yes. I figured it out after the second time half a million dollars missed from my account," I said calmly.

"What about the first time?" he asked.

"I just thought someone had hacked my passwords," I said simply.

"How did you know Mister Long had a hand in the robbery?" he asked.

"I never really trusted him. When he canceled on me a few nights ago, I knew there was something wrong. So, the next day when I heard them talking, I got a little shocked at first but then it all added up. So, I recorded their confession," I said with confidence.

He asked a few questions and tried his best to ruin me since they had nothing to lose. At the end I didn't lose a thing but they both got forty-five years in prison. As we got out of the courtroom, Ben was waiting in the hallway.

"Hey sister!" he said as he saw me.

I couldn't say a thing so I just ran to him and hugged him.

Chapter Nine

I held him as tight as I could. I was so afraid to let go of him. I was afraid of letting go and him disappearing. Tears were formed in my eyes. I was one blink away from bursting into tears.

"I've missed you so much," he said as I pulled away to look at him.

I was so mad at him but I've missed him more than that. I just wanted to hug him and tell him how hard it was for me to go through all the things I went through this year, specially without him.

I was trying my best to hold back my tears but I couldn't anymore. As the first tear dropped on my cheek, he wiped it right away.

"Don't cry! You don't want to look like a panda in your glory photos, do you?" he said.

It just made me laugh. I wiped my tears before it would ruin my makeup. I totally forgot about James and Charles. Ben didn't know Charles and I didn't know how to introduce him. Charles introduced me to his family as his girlfriend. Should I just introduce him as my boyfriend? I think so. I knew I wasn't going to introduce him as James' roommate.

"Ben, this is Charles, my boyfriend," I said.

Charles looked a little worried since Ben was the first person from my family he was meeting and probably he would be the only one. And of course, because Ben was taller and pretty stronger than Charles. But Ben was pretty nice to him. As they shook hands, I saw Charles calmed down.

Mister Smith needed to stay at the courthouse to do some paper work. As we walked out, everybody was asking questions and taking photos. I didn't know if I should've answered their questions or not. It was pretty crazy out there. We barely could get out of the courthouse.

"I was not expecting this. What should I do?" I asked Charles.

"I think it's better if we just go. You might get hurt if you stay," Charles said.

"I agree. As soon as you say the first word, they won't leave you alone," Ben said.

We hardly could get out of the crowd. They wouldn't give up. Some of them followed us for two blocks. They wanted to know what happened in the court. They were getting on my nerves.

"I say we all go back to my place and celebrate," I said.

"Awesome! I'll pick up some champagne on the way. James, you come with me?" Ben asked.

James just nodded. They took a cab and left. Charles and I got in his car and left. As I got in the car, he put his hand behind my neck and pulled me in and kissed me. I kissed him back. I really would never get tired of his gentle kisses.

"What was that for?" I asked as he pulled away.

"Just a little congratulations on your win," he said.

"Well, it wouldn't be possible without your help. So…" I said.

He pulled me in again and kissed me. I could feel his smile on my lips.

As we got to my place, I changed into something more comfortable and he took off his jacket and tie. I wore a pair of blue jeans and a plane loose white T-shirt. I took off my makeup, too. I was trying to braid my hair as I walked out of my room. Charles was sitting in the living room. I was going to the kitchen as I was still trying to braid my hair.

"Can I do that?" he asked.

"Do what?" I asked confused.

"Braid your hair," he said with a goofy smile.

"You really know how to braid?" I asked shocked.

"Yeah!" he said as his smile got even bigger.

I went back to the living room. I sat on the ground in front of him. He took his time to braid my hair perfectly. He was a professional, I could say. He didn't pull my hair too much. He didn't braid it too loose. It was perfect.

"How did you even learn how to braid so perfectly?" I asked as he was done.

I was looking at it in the mirror. It was so beautiful.

"My mom used to say there is nothing more impressive than a guy who can braid his girl's hair so she taught me and Christian," he said with a little smile on his face.

"She sounds amazing. I'd like to meet her someday," I said.

"She really was amazing! I wish she could meet you too," he said with a dimming smile.

"What do you mean?" I asked confused.

"She passed away a few years ago because of cancer," he said as there was not much of his smile left.

I just ran to him and hugged him. I held him as tight as I could. He wrapped his arms around me, too. My fingers went through his hair. It was so soft. I pulled away a little to see his face. I placed a little kiss on his lips.

"I'm so sorry. Tell me about her," I said.

"Well, she was the perfect mother. She would always talk to us about who we were dating or hanging out with. I remember when she first told us about braiding, she said she fell for our dad the day he braided her hair," he said with a smile.

"Well, it's pretty hot that you know how to braid," I said with a smirk.

I was about to kiss him but the doorbell rang. I just got up and opened the door. Ben and James were holding a lot of stuff including two bottles of champagne. They were changed into more comfortable clothes than the suits they were wearing.

"What's all these?" I asked as I couldn't help my laughter.

"Ben decided to cook so he dragged me to the grocery store," James said with a straight face.

James hated any kind of shopping. If he needed clothes or anything else and had to go shopping, it would be more like someone trying to kill him.

"And can I ask why there is so much alcohol?" I asked as I still was laughing.

"Because we're celebrating," Ben said.

He walked to me and gave a little box. It was tied with a piece of ribbon.

"Happy late birthday!" he said.

I gave him a quick hug and opened my present. It was a pair of Swarovski earrings. I gave him another hug.

"So, what do you want to cook?" I asked.

"Lasagna, of course," he said.

Everyone just started to laugh including me.

"Why does everyone know I like lasagna?" I asked.

"Because you love it more than you love me," James said.

"Well, that's not true," I said.

Charles was a little more quiet than usual. Ben popped open a bottle of champagne and we drank a toast. He was acting like nothing has happened. But it did. I knew we had to talk about it eventually but we needed to talk about it alone.

We spend the night drinking champagne and talking as Ben was cooking. He got way better in cooking than he was. But still I was kind of mad at him. I couldn't remember but as I wrote in my diaries, he didn't come to my eighteenth birthday. I remember reading in my journals about how mad I was at him for not making it to my birthday. I remember reading that if he was there something wouldn't have happened. Whatever it was I couldn't even write about it in my dairies and I think it was the reason I drank and drove that night. I just wish I could remember.

"How was your birthday anyway?" Ben asked out of nowhere.

"Actually, I can't remember it," I said.

I watched Ben as the impression on his face dropped and got replaced with a confused look.

"What do you mean that you cannot remember?" he asked confused.

And that was when I figured out, he might have no idea I've been in an accident. I couldn't quite remember if I told him about it or not. My memories after the accident have a few gaps here and there. But James and Charles were even more shocked than I was.

"Didn't anybody tell you I got into a car crash?" I asked.

"Dad told me about the accident but didn't say anything else," he said.

James and Charles left the kitchen, giving us a little privacy.

"So, you might want to sit down for this," I said and took a deep breath.

I couldn't believe my parents didn't tell him anything. It was hard for me to tell it all over again. It hasn't been even a week since I told James. It was too much for me to tell it twice within a week. I sat down and finished my drink. Ben was sitting down and ready to hear what happened to me while he was gone.

"Well, I can't quite remember it yet. I just can remember like a few pictures from the night of the accident. But I drank too much and drove and got into an accident. I just know that I was home alone and I wanted to go to Max's place. Apparently, I was mad at him for some reason. Anyway, I was in a coma for twenty days and when I got out of the coma, I couldn't remember a thing. After a month of reading my dairies and going to therapy every other day, I got most of my memories back. But I still cannot remember a month before the accident which includes my eighteenth birthday," I said.

I was choking by the end of it. While Ben was still in shock, I got up and drank some water. Ben didn't say a word. The only thing that pulled him out of his thoughts was the sound of the oven timer. I sat the table quickly. A few minutes passed and Ben didn't move a finger. I moved my hand in front of him and got his attention. But still, he didn't even say a word.

I let James and Charles know that the diner was ready. We sat and had dinner but Ben still couldn't say a thing. James, Charles and I were talking but not even a single word escaped Ben's mouth. As soon as the dinner was over and Charles and

I washed the dishes, Ben finally spoke after what seemed like an hour.

"I think I better go," Ben said and grabbed his coat and left.

We were all shocked. The only thing I could think of was to ask James to go after him.

"James, can you make sure he gets to his hotel room safe and sound?" I asked James.

"Sure," he said, grabbed his coat and ran after Ben.

I couldn't believe what just happened. I already got a headache and it was getting worse and worse. I just went to the living room and threw myself on the couch. Charles was even more confused than I was. He sat beside me and wrapped an arm around me and pulled me in. I leaned in and buried myself in the comfort of his arms.

We stayed quiet for a while. I wasn't in the mood for talking. He probably didn't know what to say. It was so weird. I've never seen Ben like this before. The only thing that was keeping me a little calm was the fact that James went after him.

After like an hour or so, my phone rang. I jumped as I heard it ringing. I picked up quickly. It was James, hopefully with a news from Ben.

"James? Are you with him? Is he okay?" I asked as I picked up.

"He's still a little shocked but he's okay. He took a pill and went to bed. I'm going to stay with him tonight. I don't think he should be alone," he said.

"Thank you! He didn't happen to say anything, did he?" I asked.

"He could barely say a complete sentence. Do you have any idea what's wrong with him?" he asked.

"I wish I knew. Maybe something happened that I still can't remember but I'm not sure," I said.

"Okay! I'll talk to you later. And if Charles is still there, tell him I won't be home," he said.

"Okay!" I said and hung up.

"Is Ben all right?" Charles finally spoke.

"I don't know. James will stay with him tonight," I said.

I buried myself in his chest again. He wrapped his arms around me. It was so comfortable and homey. It was getting late and I didn't know if he would stay here or leave me alone. I really wished he didn't. I felt like I couldn't be left alone right now.

"Charles, you stay here tonight?" I looked up at him as I asked.

"Do you want me to?" he asked.

I just nodded instead.

"Sure baby. But I hope you have something that would fit me," he said.

"Actually, I might have something!" I said.

I got up and went to my bedroom and Charles followed me. I knew I had something that was way too big for me but I wasn't sure if it would fit Charles or not. I bought a few pairs of sweatpants a while ago and I ordered one of them in the wrong size. And since I have too many big T-shirts, I thought I could find Charles something.

I gave him the clothes and he went to the bathroom to change. When he came out, I got amazed. They fit him perfectly.

"Just tell me they aren't that bastard's clothes!" he said.

"Actually, they are mine. I threw away all of that bastard's stuff," I said with a smirk.

He walked to me and kissed me. As I was kissing him, I got on to my toes to reach his height. I ran my fingers through his hair and pulled him a little down. His hands were on my back. He was pulling me closer and closer to him. As our bodies were about to be against each other, he stopped which was somehow good. I couldn't sleep with him tonight.

He let go of my waist and kissed my forehead before going to bed. I changed, too and went to bed. As I laid down, he pulled me a little closer to him and wrapped me in his arms. I was pretty tired and a little drunk so it didn't take long for me to fall asleep in the comfort of his arms.

Chapter Ten

I woke with the sound of pouring rain. Charles was already awake. He was still holding me close in his arms. It was still pretty early. It was just before seven and I really didn't know why the hell I woke up now. Maybe it's because of the cold.

"Morning!" I said.

"Morning baby!" he said and placed a kiss on my cheek.

I crawled more into his arms and he covered us with the blanket. I was so cold. I didn't know why my apartment felt like a freezer. It's usually warm and cozy. After a few minutes of trying to warm myself up, I got up to go check on the radiator. For some reason I didn't know, the temperature was pretty low. Ben must have turned it down as always. I turned it back up.

I went back to my room to go to the bathroom. As I went in, Charles was sitting on my bed and drying his face with a towel. His hair was a little wet. It was falling on his face. I messed up his hair a little more before I walked into the bathroom.

As I went to the kitchen to make something for breakfast, I heard a Christmas song playing. Charles must have connected his phone to the speakers. I turned it down a little. Charles was a little shocked. Who would turn down a happy Christmas song? Well, I would. Christmas didn't mean anything to me.

"Do you like hot chocolate?" I asked.

"Is there anybody who doesn't like it?" he asked.

He was right. Who doesn't love chocolate? But it was like Christmas. Everybody loved it expect for me. Why? Well, I was always alone at home with Ben. And for the last few years, he would just come back for me so I wouldn't be all alone.

Charles turned it up a little as a Taylor Swift song came up. It was too happy for me. I just continued with what I was doing and making some chocolate chip pancakes. He was singing with it. It was somehow cute. He had a good voice.

"Can you just turn it down a little?" I asked as it was finished.

"Why? It's so happy and Christmassy!" he said.

"Well, I'm not a big fan of Christmas," I said as I poured some batter into the pan.

He gasped. He was looking at me with wide eyes. His jaw dropped after a few seconds.

"You don't like Christmas?" he asked as he was trying to catch his breath.

I just nodded and didn't say a thing.

"Why? It's the most wonderful time of the year. Presents under the tree and hot coco milk in the morning. It's so magical," he said exited.

"Well, not for me! I literally can't remember any Christmas morning waking up to such thing. I remember being alone at home with Ben as always. My parents were always working and if they weren't, which happened only once or twice, we would go to London. And even then, we couldn't spend much time with them," I said.

He pinned me to the counter with his hands on my sides and kissed my lips softly. His lips already tasted like chocolate. I put my hands on his face and kissed him a little deeper before pulling back.

"Well, that's going to change. You're coming to my parents' with me this year," he said.

I was about to say no but as I opened my mouth, he put a finger on my lips and didn't let me even start.

"I'd really love to show you a real Christmas," he said.

My lips curled into a smiled under his finger. I really wanted to know what would Christmas be like out of my bedroom.

"Okay!" I said.

He put a little kiss on my cheek and took the pancakes out of the pan before they'd burn.

"So, tell me a little about this Christmas thing. What should I expect?" I said as we were eating breakfast.

"First of all, we're going out of town. It's just a little farm and a cute house. We'd go there the day before Christmas and we decorate the tree and put our presents under it. But my dad usually throws a huge party in New York for the New Year's Eve. Would you be my date?" he asked.

"Sure, why not!" I said with a huge goofy smile.

I didn't know why but it really felt like I finally was going to have a family. I always felt like a rich orphan. But now I felt like I belonged somewhere, even though we haven't been to an actual date yet. I didn't know what was so special about Charles but when I'm with him, it feels like home. It feels like I found where I belong after eighteen years.

"So, what should I get your family?" I asked.

"You don't need to get them anything," he said.

"But isn't it a Christmas tradition to give presents or something?" I asked not sure if I remembered it right or not.

"Well, yeah! But you don't have to," he said.

I just smiled and didn't say or asked anything else. I didn't know how old was Charlotte but she was a pretty girl with a good sense of fashion. I thought I could get her a necklace or a bracelet. Christian was Charles' twin and they actually looked a lot alike. I could say they had a lot of fun pranking others when they were younger.

"So, I was thinking, what do you think about going out tonight? Like our first date," he asked and pulled me out of my thoughts.

"Yeah, that sounds nice," I said with a smile.

"Then I'll pick you up at seven. And you might want to wear a dress," he said with a smirk.

We ate the rest of our breakfast in silence. I was still thinking about what I could get Christian and his dad. I was going back and forth between tie or watch or cufflinks. Worse than that was that I didn't know what to get Charles. I know it hasn't been even a week but it feels like a lot more. I dated Nick for almost four months and I didn't know him like I know Charles now.

Charles left a little while after breakfast. He needed to head to the office. I called Ben a few times but he didn't pick up and then James called me after a few minutes.

"Hey! How's Ben?" I asked as I picked up.

"He's still a little shocked," he said.

"Can he talk?" I asked.

"I don't know," he said.

"Okay! I'll come over," I said.

"I don't know if it's a good idea or not," he said.

"James, He wasn't there for me when I needed him but I'm not going to leave him alone," I said.

I hung up and got changed. I wore a pair of navy-blue jeans, a red knitted sweater, a yellow waterproof coat and a pair of red boots. I grabbed a bag and put everything I needed in it.

It was nearly noon when I got there. As I walked into his suite, I got shocked. He was laying on the bed, still with his last night's clothes on. He was half awake and half asleep.

"James? What's going on?" I asked.

"I wish I knew," he said.

I went to him and sat on his bed. He barely could open his eyes. I put my hand on his shoulder and shook him a little. He opened his eyes a little more.

"Brooke, I'm so sorry. I should've come back for you! It's all my fault," he said.

I didn't know what he was talking about but I couldn't watch him like that. So, I decided to let it go and try to make him a little better.

"Ben, it's not your fault. It's nobody's fault. Okay?" I said.

"But if I came back for your birthday…" he said.

"It's gone now! I'm okay. You shouldn't beat yourself up over it," I said.

"Brooke I can't live with myself like this," he said.

"Sure, you can. Whatever happened is in the past. I'm okay now and you can't beat yourself up over it forever," I said again.

He didn't say another word. He just nodded.

"Come on. Take a shower and get some sleep," I said and helped him get up.

He took a shower and slept and James and I left. James went back home and I went shopping. I knew I had clothes for tonight but I needed some clothes for the Christmas.

I spent a few hours looking around and hoped to find something for presents but I really couldn't. It was already Tuesday, and Christmas was on Friday which meant I only had like two days to shop. It was getting hopeless. Finally, I decided to go to Cartier to get Charles a watch. As I was there, I saw a ring and loved it instantly so I bought it for Charlotte. I got a few things for myself as well.

I knew it was getting late and I needed to go home. But then I remembered there is a place nearby that sells Persian handmade silk ties. So, I went there and got two gift boxes for Christian and his dad. They had matching tie, handkerchief and cufflinks.

It was passed four when I got home. I took a quick shower and straightened my hair. I put on a full glam makeup with red lipstick. I wore a red strapless dress with red high heels. It wasn't long enough to cover the scar on my leg but I didn't care about it anymore. Charles would see it sooner or later.

I called Ben a couple of times but he didn't pick up. He probably was still asleep since he wasn't so good. I was worried about him. I have never seen him like this before.

My doorbell rang exactly at seven. I wore my overcoat before opening the door. I wanted to see his expression in the restaurant since my dress was pretty revealing. As I opened the door I got amazed by how handsome and hot he looked. He was wearing a gray suit, a patterned gray tie and a freshly ironed white shirt.

"Hi!" I said as soon as I could speak.

"Hi! Are you ready?" he asked.

I just nodded and closed the door behind me. He held his arm for me to hold so I did. We were kind of awkwardly silent the whole way to the restaurant. As we got there, he got out of the car and opened the door for me.

When we got in the restaurant and I took off my overcoat, his jaw dropped. It took him a few seconds to pull himself back together. We sat down and had a classic first date. He was really gentle and polite but his eyes were a little wilder than they usually were. We ate and talked for the entire night. We had a couple of glasses of wine but he was still pretty sober.

He drove me back home. I didn't know how to invite him back to my place like a lady. Did I really need a reason? I didn't know actually. He might have been sober but I was a glass away from being completely drunk. That was it. A drink!

"Do you want to come up for a drink?" I asked.

"Sure," he said.

And that was just the beginning of the night.

Chapter Eleven

I grabbed two wine glasses and a bottle of red wine and went back to the living room. I sat on the couch and crossed my right leg over the left one. It made my dress go up a little and revealed more of my scar. Charles looked at it like it was the first time he saw it but didn't say anything. I opened the bottle and poured it in the glasses.

"Cheers!" I said and rose my glass.

"So, how was I on a date?" He asked after a few sips.

"Pretty charming and handsome. You really know how to dress for a date," I said with a smirk.

He didn't say a thing and just smirked. Glasses of wine got drank one after the other. I drank two and was completely drunk but not in the way that I could pass out. I think Charles drank three or four. He was pretty drunk too. His eyes were getting wilder and wilder from the beginning of the night.

"Can I ask about your scar?" he asked.

"It's just a gift from the accident," I said and laughed.

He put his hand on it and followed it a little up under my dress. His touch was sending shivers down my body. He took away his hand after a few seconds. He was looking at me in silence, just looking. I drank the last sip of my glass and put the glass on the coffee table. He was still looking at me in silence.

There was a piece of hair fallen on my chest. He brushed

it out of my chest and put it behind my shoulder. He didn't take away his hand. It went down to my bare back to my waist and to my lower back. He was killing me. He pulled me closer as he moved a little closer. He put his other hand on my face but still didn't do anything.

My lips parted as his thumb moved closed to my lips. He brushed his thumb on my bottom lip. He was torturing me. His hand slid to the back of my neck and pulled me closer. We were just a few inches apart. My eyes closed subconsciously as my lips parted more. He put his lips on mine and kissed me.

I kissed him back as I ran my fingers through his hair and pulled him towards myself. I leaned backward as I pulled him toward myself. Our tongues were tied together. It wasn't enough. I wanted more. I needed more. I bit his bottom lip and pulled it a little. He pulled away a little and then went down to my neck.

I threw back my head in pleasure. He was a little less gentle than the last time. He was wilder, more turned on. His hand went down to my thigh and laid me on the couch as he was kissing my neck. A moan escaped my mouth. He pulled away for a second to see my face then kissed me down to my chest.

As nice as it was, he was torturing me. My dress was too tight to do anything in it. All I could do to make it less torturing was to push my thighs together. He was holding his weight with one arm and the other one was on my thigh. I slid my hand down his back and pulled him down closer to me.

My back arched as his hand slid down my thigh to the back of my knee. I couldn't take it anymore. I already was so wet. I was shaking under his touch. I pulled him up to kiss his lips. His hair was so messy. He was looking sexier than ever.

I kissed him roughly and pulled him closer a little more. His hand went a little up under my dress. It was burning my skin so bad I thought it would leave a scar.

I broke the kiss and sat up on the couch. I grabbed his hand and got up. I dragged him to my bedroom and closed the door. As I turned around, he pinned me to the door and attacked my lips. I grabbed his tie and pulled him closer. Since I was still wearing my high heels he didn't need to bend down too much.

I untied his tie and threw it on the ground. I undone the buttons one by one. He kicked of his shoes. I was still completely dressed. I took off his shirt and threw it somewhere on the ground. I pushed him back till we were in front of my bed. His hand found the zipper of my dress and pulled it down slowly. As he took his hand off of my body, my dress fell down on the ground and left me in my panties.

I wasn't wearing a bra underneath my dress. His eyes got wilder as he saw my body. I kicked away my dress with my foot before it would get ruined under our feet. I sat on the bed and pulled him towards myself. I was only wearing a pair of black laced panties and my heels. I took off his pants and left him in his tight black boxers.

He put his hand on my face and kissed my lips as he laid me down on the bed. He kissed me down to my neck, my breasts, my belly to my thigh and my scar. I couldn't take it anymore. I was running out of breath. I pulled him back up and wrapped my legs around his waist and pulled him down.

After a few kissed, he got up and grabbed a condom before taking his boxers off. He took off my panties slowly and kissed me there. As his lips touched me, a loud moan escaped my mouth. I gripped the sheets to keep myself from moving.

He kissed my lips before thrusting into me. I wrapped my legs around his waist and pulled him towards me. He was moving back and forth in me gently. I moaned a few times in pleasure. His lips didn't leave mine. He moaned deeply on my lips. He was holding most of his weight with his arms while my hands were on his back pulling him down. A loud moan escaped my lips as I came. He kept moving till he came, too. He sighed as he came and pulled out of me.

He covered us with the blanket. I kicked off my shoes and crawled into his arms. We stayed quiet for a while. The only sound that could be heard was the sound of rain pouring down and our unsteady breathings.

After a while, I grabbed a sheet and wrapped around my body. He grabbed my hand before I could get up.

"Where are you going?" he asked confused.

"I just want to take off my makeup," I said with a smile.

"Can I do it?" he asked excited.

"Sure!" I said.

I got up and grabbed a makeup remover wipe. I gave it to him and laid down on the bed. He started to wipe off my makeup. He was so gentle. It was so nice to lay down and someone remove your makeup for you. I slowly fell asleep while he was still removing my makeup.

I opened my eyes and didn't know where I was at first. After looking around, I figured I was in my old bedroom. My hands were tied behind my back. I tried to move but I couldn't. I was too sore. I was completely naked. I looked down at my body and saw bruises everywhere. My body was wet and cold. I could hear someone breathe behind me but I couldn't turn around. My legs and back was so sore that I couldn't move. I was freaking out. I wanted to shout and scream but as I opened my mouth, not a single sound escaped.

I woke up in the middle of the night, covered in sweat. I was shaking so badly that Charles would wake up any second. I slid away from his arms and sat on the edge of my bed. I was feeling so sick. What the hell did I just see? What the hell was that? A dream? A nightmare? Some sort of memory from my past? Why did it feel so real?

The more I thought about it the sicker I got. I wrapped a sheet around myself and ran to the bathroom to throw up. I closed the door behind me but didn't lock it. I didn't think Charles would wake up. But as I was throwing up, he came in and held my hair back. He rubbed my back a little and I threw up even more.

I sat on the bathroom floor as there was nothing left in my stomach to throw up. My body was covered in sweat. I was still shaking from the dream. Charles looked scared as hell. He was holding my hands, waiting for me to say something but I still couldn't find my voice to say a word or even a simple thank you.

"Brooke? Are you all right?" he asked.

I just shook my head no in return. I couldn't find my voice yet.

"What happened? Is there anything I can do?" he asked.

His voice was starting to shake. I was freaking him out. I gathered all my strength to speak.

"It was just a nightmare," I said.

My voice was so low that I thought he didn't hear me at first. He just pulled me in his arms. We sat there on the bathroom floor for a while.

"Do you want to take a shower or a bath?" he asked after

a few minutes.

I was so tired but it wasn't such a bad idea. I really needed to wash up after what I just saw so I just nodded. He helped me to get up. I turned on the water in the bathtub and tied my hair into a bun.

"Can you help me?" I asked as I got in the tub.

He nodded and took off his boxers and joined me in the bathtub. I could fall asleep any second in the tub. He helped me wash up. As I got out of the tub, he took a quick shower himself and got out. We got dressed and went back to bed.

I woke up around noon with the worst headache possible. Charles wasn't in the bed but the smell of bacon and coffee was coming from the kitchen. I got up and before heading to the kitchen, went to the bathroom. I was feeling less sick. But the headache was worse.

"Oh, you're the best," I said as I walked into the kitchen.

I hugged him. He kissed my forehead.

"Good morning, babe. How did you sleep?" he asked.

"It was okay," I said with a smile.

I wasn't lying. I didn't say it was perfect but it was okay. He placed a plate in front of me full of bacon and eggs and toasts and poured me a cup of coffee.

"Do you think I can eat this much?" I asked and laughed.

"Well, you should. You need it," he said and sat at the island.

"Why would I?" I asked, still laughing.

"Because we're going shopping," he said.

"Shopping for what?" I asked.

Didn't he shop for presents yet? That's impossible. I didn't mind go shopping. I'd liked to buy some new clothes.

"For Christmas!" he said.

I just stared at him with wide eyes.

"I got my gifts but I wanted to buy a new suit and tie and stuff," he said.

"Actually, I wanted to go shopping for some new clothes, too. I couldn't get myself anything yesterday," I said

"You went shopping yesterday?" he asked.

"Yeah! I went to see Ben and I had a few hours left till you'd pick me up so I went shopping for gifts," I said.

"Did you really get gifts for my family?" he asked like he couldn't believe I did.

"Yeah!" I said like it was the most obvious thing in the world.

"Aww! You really didn't have to," he said.

"I know! I just like giving gifts," I said with a smile.

"Can I see them?" he asked.

"Nope!" I said.

We finished our breakfast as he kept asking me if he could see the gifts I got for his family. We dressed and headed out. I wore a pair of black jeans, a lavender hoodie, black waterproof coat and black boots. He even braided my hair so it wouldn't get messy in the rain.

We went to Charles's apartment and he got changed, too. He matched his outfit with mine except that he wore a purple hoodie. We spent hours shopping. I got a couple of dresses since we might be going to a few of parties according to Charles. And he got a few new suits and ties. I showed him where I got his father's and Christian's gifts from at the end. He got a couple of ties and handkerchiefs there. They were pretty different from the ones I got for them. They had more simple patterns. But the ones he bought was so colorful and simply happier.

We ate dinner at a little diner like any other two young people who are dating. Last night was nice too but when a few paparazzi appeared as we were leaving the restaurant, it somehow got ruined. But here nobody would bother us.

As I got home, it was past eleven. I was supper tired. Charles went back to his apartment since he needed to take care of some stuff the next morning. I just changed and went to bed. I didn't brush my hair or anything. I kept the braid. It was still pretty nice and in place.

Chapter Twelve

I was standing in the corner and watching my guests leave one by one. I knew as soon as they were gone, my freedom would be gone, too. Max was going to propose to me tonight. Not that he wanted to. He had to. I heard my parents whispering about it the other day. I didn't want to get married. I wasn't even in love with him. But I had to say yes. It was the only way that I wouldn't start a war.

I still don't know why our grandfathers wanted us to get married. Well, they wanted their children to get married but they both had sons and neither were gay! So, they decided that Max and I should get married. But why so soon? We were both only eighteen. We didn't know anything about life.

It was so cruel. I liked Max but I was never in love with him. And now I have to say yes to his proposal. He wasn't happy about it either. He was drinking way too much tonight and he didn't spend a second with me. He was banging some girl I didn't know.

Yes. He cheated on me time after time and I even caught him a couple of times myself. But we didn't break up. Why? Because we couldn't. It was decided for us to be together. We had no power over our families to get out of this.

I drank the rest of my beer and locked the doors since everyone was gone and my parents wouldn't be home tonight. I just laid on the couch and closed my eyes. I wished I'd fall asleep right away. I didn't want to get engaged tonight. It was horrifying.

"Don't sleep," he said seriously.

I opened my eyes but still didn't move. He came closer and grabbed my hand and pulled me up from the couch. I was a little dizzy since I drank a little too much. He reached into his pocket and took out a ring. It was beautiful but I still hated it. He just held it in front of me. He didn't get on his knee or anything. He just stood there.

"Will you marry me?" he asked with no emotion in his voice.

His face was completely straight. I wanted to say no but my dad would kill me. I knew that for sure. And if he wouldn't, Max's father would kill me.

"Yes," I said with a straight face.

He just slipped the ring in my finger and left. I sat on the couch for a few minutes before going to my bedroom. I wanted to sleep. I needed to sleep. I was too tired to stay up for any longer.

As I walked into my room, I found it colder than ever. It felt so strange. I shivered as a cold wind came through the window. I closed it and turned on my nightlight just to see where I was going. I kicked off my shoes. As my feet touched the soft carpet in my room, the pain in my feet disappeared. Which only made me feel the pain in my heart even more.

I grabbed a wipe and removed my makeup. As I was trying to unzip my dress, Max walked in. He put his hands on my shoulders for a second and then unzipped my dress. As he took his hands off of my back, my dress fell on the ground. He put his hands back on my shoulders and slid them to my waist. I didn't know what he was up to but I had a feeling it was no good.

As I wanted to get away, he grabbed me by my waist, turned me around and lifted me up on his shoulder. I was in shock. As he threw me on my bed, I screamed in pain. He knew it pretty well that if he'd even hold my hand a little tight, it would hurt me and I would get bruises. Maybe I was just too weak.

As I was still in too much pain to move or even open my eyes, he took of his clothes and cuffed my hands. As I felt the cold steel against my wrists, my eyes opened. I was looking at him in shock. What the hell he was up to?

"What are you doing?" I asked, too scared to actually know the answer.

"We're going to have a little fun, fiancé!" he said.

He kissed me roughly and then bit my bottom lip. It wasn't a gentle turning on bite. It was a harsh scary painful bite. I tried to kick him away but he was way stronger than I was and I was too drunk to be able to gather all my strength. All I could think of was to hit him in the head with my hands and since they were cuffed together, I thought maybe the handcuff could help out.

But as soon as I move my hands, he read my mind and held my hands above my head. He was looking at me with the most evil eyes I have ever seen in my life. He wasn't smirking as most of the time. He was just furious. He got on top of me and locked me down with his legs. He took my hands, uncuffed one and then cuffed me to my headboard.

He bent down and kissed me again. I was disgusted. I was scared. My body was shivering from the fear under him. I didn't know what was next. I was scared to death from it.

He put his hands on my breasts and squeezed them. As he

sighed, I felt sick. He was pressing him to me and I could feel him getting harder and harder. I shot my eyes closed. I didn't want to see him. It wasn't fun. It was a sick game that only a rapist could play.

As he sucked down my neck, I felt disgusted. I was pressing my thighs together to keep him from entering me. His hands were still on my breasts, squeezing them. As his hands slid down my hips and thighs, I froze. He spread my legs more than I could. I cried in pain.

"Please stop. You're hurting me." I begged him as tears streamed down my face.

"Oh honey, I'm just getting started," he said with a disgusting tone.

He grabbed the back of my knees and lifted my legs up. He slid away my panties and thrusted his fingers in me. He watched me cry more and more as he moved his fingers in me. I was suffering and yet my body was responding to his touch. I didn't think I'd come but I did. It didn't matter. I was getting raped by my fiancé and there was nothing I could do.

I couldn't catch my breath since I was crying and sobbing. I couldn't even open my eyes anymore if I wanted to. I was too scared of the sight. I just could feel his hands and lips on me. He let go of my legs and let them fall on the mattress. He slid down my panties. He spread my legs again.

"Please stop." I begged again.

But he didn't listen. He didn't even respond. He just entered me in the most painful way possible. I screamed out in pain. But he couldn't care less.

I was feeling less conscious than before. I felt like I would pass out any second. I didn't even mind dying right now. I just wanted not to feel a damn thing.

As he was holding me down by my waist, he thrusted me time after time, harder and harder. He kept on going till I came but he didn't stop. He was still going. My body couldn't take it anymore and I just passed out under him.

Chapter Thirteen

I woke up covered in sweat. My heart was beating so fast and unsteady. As I sat up on my bed, I felt sick. I ran to the bathroom and threw up. I couldn't understand what was happening to me. I just knew that it might not be just a bad dream. It felt so real. I could still feel his hands on me.

I knew he was my ex-boyfriend but I didn't know if what I just saw was the truth about my past or not. As I thought about it more and more, I got sick again. I threw up until there was nothing left in my stomach. I sat there on the bathroom floor, trying my best to figure out everything. But after about an hour I got nowhere.

I couldn't even breathe properly anymore. I needed some fresh air. I just got up and wore something comfortable and warm and got out of my apartment. I didn't know where I was going. I just knew I needed fresh air.

I was walking for about half an hour without a destination. I just walked and walked and walked but as I got where I had my accident, I stopped. I knew for sure I couldn't remember it. My therapist brought me here a few times but I couldn't remember. But I could now. I remembered it to the last detail. Even when I hit the sings and the lights, to the second that I passed out.

I was standing across from the street and just stared at the spot I had my accident. They had changed the lights and the signs. I felt like I couldn't breathe. My heart was pounding in my chest and my head was spinning around. Before I knew it, I fell on the ground. I wasn't unconscious yet. I could hear people talking around me and calling nine-one-one.

I woke up in the hospital, alone, laying on a bed. My head hurt so bad. I still felt sick. I found my phone in my pocket. Before I could do anything, a doctor came in.

"Oh, good. You're awake!" he said with a smile.

He looked too young to be a doctor. Maybe a nurse?

"Can you tell me what is wrong with me?" I asked straight away, hopeless to find an answer to all of this.

"Well, you passed out in the middle of the street," he said.

"I mean do you know why I passed out in the street?" I asked annoyed.

Wow! For a doctor he was kind of dumb.

"Well, your blood test should be back any minute. I can tell you then. Who do you want us to call to pick you up?" he asked.

"Can't I just go myself?" I asked and he shook his head no.

I called James myself to ask him to pick me up at the hospital. He didn't ask why I was there. He just said he'd be here soon. I knew I could call Charles or even Ben but I wasn't ready to face neither of them. Especially not Ben.

He knew what happened to me. He knew I was raped. I called him the next day. He didn't pick up but I left a message. He must have heard it. If not, then why would he say it was all his fault? He heard it but was too much an asshole to call me. I expected more from him.

After a while the doctor from earlier came back but he was not alone. He came back with my doctor and my dad and

Ben. It was a full package of betrayal. How could they even show their faces here? My dad, the one who didn't even let me talk when I told him something horrible happened the night of my birthday. My dear brother, Ben, who didn't even bother to call me after I was raped, the one who didn't return my calls for months. And my dear doctor, Doctor Benson who didn't give a shit about my condition.

"Wow. The full package is here! Are you here to let me down even more?" I asked as I sat up on my bed.

"How are you feeling Miss Edwards?" Doctor Benson asked.

"How do I feel? Well, I just got my memories back and remembered what really happened in that month. Oh, actually there was only ten days that really mattered," I said and let out a deep breath.

Ben went pale and my dad had no idea what I was talking about. Sure, he didn't. He never knew what was happening in my life.

"Ben? Do you care to tell the story or should I?" I asked.

Ben couldn't even catch a breath. Did he think I would never get my memories back?

"Dad? Do you remember when I told you something horrible happened the night of my birthday? Do you remember what you said? You said you're sure they can get the stain out of my dress. You thought I spilled something on my dress. But no Dad. I got raped that night. The one who you always wanted to be your son-in-law raped me. But you would know that if you cared enough to let me finish but instead, you walked away," I said and took a deep breath before continuing.

"I called Ben after you left. He didn't pick up for God knows why, so I left a message. I told him everything to the last detail I could remember. But he didn't call me back. He didn't even send me a single text. Dad? Didn't you even noticed I locked myself in the house for days and slept in the living room on the couch?" I was shouting at him, not caring if anyone could hear me.

Fortunately, they had closed the door as they came in so whomever heard me didn't know it was me. I didn't want to be recorded because if it happened, the video would end up on the internet and Charles or a member of his family would find out and I really didn't want him to find out, at least not now, not this way.

"How can you call yourself a father?" I asked with no emotion in my voice.

They were quiet for some time till Ben decided it was time to ask the doctors to leave us alone. They left but I kind of wished they didn't. I could feel my blood temperature rising and I knew it could be dangerous especially for someone like me in this delicate situation.

"Brooke, I am so sorry. I know I should have called you but I couldn't face the fact that if had come back, it wouldn't have happened to you." Ben said as he was walking to me.

"Oh, you couldn't face that? I couldn't walk into my room and not see his fucking face." I shouted at him.

My throat was starting to hurt but I couldn't keep calm anymore. I felt like I was going crazy. My dad sat on a chair and held his head in his hands. Ben stayed quiet for some time. The younger doctor came back after a few minutes of complete silence.

"Can I come in?" he asked as he opened the door a little bit. I nodded slightly.

"Well, there is nothing unusual in your test. You mostly

passed out because of low blood sugar and the shock of getting your memories back. There is nothing to be worried about," he said.

As the doctor explained everything to me, my dad left the room but Ben stayed. As the doctor was leaving, James came in. Both Ben and James were shocked and confused as they saw each other.

"Thanks, James, for picking me up," I said as I got up from the bed.

They were both still quiet but Ben knew why I called him.

"Please take care of her." Ben said as we were walking out of the room.

As we went to sign some papers and pay, they told us we just need to sign a few papers since my dad had already paid. As we got a cab to my place, James started to ask questions.

"Brooke? What happened? Why were you even in the hospital? Why was your dad crying in the hallway?" he asked without giving me a second to answer.

"Can we talk about it at home?" I asked.

He just nodded. I ordered lunch on the way since it was nearly noon and I haven't eaten all day. As we got home, he started to ask question.

"Brooke? What is going on?" he asked.

"You might want to sit for this," I said and sat on the couch.

He sat down but still couldn't sit still. He was getting more and more worried. I could see it in his eyes.

"I got my memories back," I said and took a deep breath.

"Isn't it a good thing?" he asked.

"I wish it was but no, it's not. I remembered what happened that led me to drinking a bottle of twenty-year-old wine and driving to my ex's house," I said and took a deep breath before saying what happened to me or actually what he did to me.

"James, Max raped me the night of my birthday. Or should I say ten days before the accident happened," I said and let out my breath I didn't even notice I was holding.

The fact that he was my fiancé hurt me even more. Our parents always wanted us to be together, get married and have kids. It was more like a business deal than a marriage. They wanted to unite their companies and couldn't think of a better way.

He couldn't say a word. His jaw dropped as I said what happened. He couldn't talk for about ten minutes. I got up and grabbed him a glass of water. He took a few sips before he could talk.

"He raped you?" he asked breathlessly.

I just nodded and he couldn't say another word for several minutes.

"James? Can you say something?" I asked.

"I don't even know what to say!" he said.

"Who knows about it?" he asked after a few minutes of silence.

"Well, Ben was the only one who knew till this morning but now my dad and my dear doctor know, too. Why?" I asked.

"I just wanted to know," he said but he was lying.

I knew him better than this. Ben must have said something the other night. James doesn't ask these things randomly. There must be something.

"How did he even know?" he asked a little confused.

"I called him the day after my birthday. He didn't pick up so I left a message and told him everything. After that, he neither called me back nor answered my calls," I said.

As our lunch arrived, we sat and ate in silence which I somehow needed. As we were eating, I got a text from Charles saying he'd pick me up at six. I totally forgot about Christmas and his parents' country house. I ate the rest of my lunch as fast as I could. I needed to take a shower. Charles couldn't see me smelling like hospital. There was no way I could tell him what happened, not that I thought it would change how he sees me but I knew that I was not ready to tell him I was raped.

James still couldn't talk. I just left him in the living room. I took a shower as fast I could. I had about four hours to get ready and pack but there was a little problem that I had no idea what I should pack. I didn't even know how long we would be there.

I blow dried and straightened my hair as I got out of the shower. I didn't need a headache right now. I didn't know if James was still here or not so I went back to the living room. He was still there, still and quiet.

"James? Are you okay?" I asked as I sat down on the couch.

"Are you?" he asked.

"I really don't know. But I know I don't have any time to spend over thinking about it. I just know that I have only a few hours to get ready to spend Christmas at Charles' parents'," I said.

"Wait. What? You're going to his parents' country house?" he asked in shock.

"Yeah!" I said.

"If you don't want him to find out, you better put on a perfect fake face on." He suggested.

"Why?" I asked confused.

I knew he could find out there is something wrong with me but why James was suggesting a perfect fake face?

"Because he knows you pretty good and as soon as he sees you, he will figure out something horrible happened. Unless you want to tell him," he said.

"No, I can't tell him now! I haven't even figured it out myself. I can't tell him," I said.

"I know it's too much for you but you can do this. I'm not saying this because of him. I'm saying it because I love you so much," he said and pulled me in his arms.

"I love you, too jackass!" I said.

He held me for a few minutes before letting go.

"Do you think you'll be all right on your own?" he asked.

"Yeah!" I asked.

He kissed my forehead and left. I sat there in the living room for a while, trying to figure everything out. I couldn't deal with my memories right now. I went back to my bedroom and started packing. I packed everything I was sure about. I was about to call Charles to asked how long we would be there when I felt a killing pain in my stomach.

I thought it wouldn't be my period but it was. It was hitting me a good week earlier than it should. I should have expected it. I was in too much stress and pain. I ran to a pharmacy nearby to get some pills and stuff. Since I didn't have much time left, I called Charles as I was getting home from the pharmacy. He picked up after a few rings.

"Hey! How are you?" he asked as he picked up.

"Hi. I'm fine. How are you?" I asked and tried to sound normal.

"I'm good. So, are you packed yet?" he asked.

"Actually, that's why I called. How long are we going to

stay there?" I asked.

"Probably three days. Why?" he asked.

"Because I had no idea what to pack or how much to pack. Should I bring a dress or something?" I asked.

"I don't know! Actually, bring one. My dad might throw a party at the last minute," he said.

"Okay," I said.

As I got home it was already past four. I packed as fast as I could and as complete as I could. It was getting even colder than the last few days. I threw my clothes from this morning in the washing machine as I was packing. I didn't want anything in my apartment to smell like hospital.

Charles came a few minutes after six. As we got on the road the pain in my stomach got worse. Charles noticed it quickly.

"Brooke? Are you okay?" he asked.

"Yeah. It's just the annoying pain of my period," I said.

"Why don't you take a painkiller?" he asked.

"Actually, I forgot to take one," I said.

I took a painkiller. It was pretty strong. After about half an hour I fell asleep in the car.

Chapter Fourteen

"Brooke? Wake up! It's Christmas," Charles said as he shook me awake.

I could barely open my eyes. It was pretty early. The sun has just risen. It was still snowing outside.

"Good morning baby," he said and kissed my cheek.

"Good morning," I said as I messed up his hair.

It was already messy so he wouldn't mind. He brushed his hair out of his face with his fingers. He already looked perfect. My hair was the worst. The weather was not my friend last night and it made my hair all curly and they weren't the good kind of curls.

"Come on! Everyone's up," he said.

He gave me a pair Christmassy pajamas last night to wear this morning. He was already wearing his. He looked pretty adorable. I got out of the bed and got ready to go downstairs but my hair was killing me. I couldn't do anything with it so I just put into a bun so I could avoid it.

We went downstairs and everyone was already in the living room waiting for us. As I saw them, I got shocked. Charles didn't just get me matching pajamas with him, he got me a match to his family's. It was so sweet of him. His dad had made some hot chocolate milk and coffee.

As we sat down, Charlotte started to pick the presents one at a time and handing us our presents. I sneaked my presents there last night after everyone went to sleep. I really didn't expect to get any presents but his family had got me a beautiful necklace and Charles got me a watch. It was so pretty.

They liked the gifts I got them or at least they said so. Charles tried on his watch right away. By the smile on his face, I could say he really liked it. After we opened our presents and drank our coffee and hot chocolate milk, we all went to the kitchen to make breakfast. Well, not all of us. Charles's dad went outside to get some firewood for the fireplace.

Charles asked me to make some chocolate chip pancakes. Charlotte and Christian got shocked that Charles knew I can make chocolate chip pancakes. As I was making them, Charles untied my hair and brushed it with his fingers before braiding my hair.

"Are you sure you guys just met like a week ago?" Christian asked.

Charlotte laughed at how Christian was curious.

"I met him eight days ago. I think he knew me for like four months!" I said with a smile.

"Okay, it's starting to look like an old movie." Christian said with a little laughter.

"James told me a lot about her before I met her," Charles explained.

"Oh, how's James? We haven't seen him in like forever," Charlotte finally spoke.

"He's good. I think he was going to see Ben today," Charles said.

As he said, I felt something dropped in my chest. Why the hell would he want to spent his Christmas with Ben? Didn't he hear what I told him yesterday?

"What?" I asked confused.

"Who's Ben?" Charlotte asked curiously.

"Ben is Brooke's brother. He said they should take care of some business. He sounded weird actually," Charles said.

I had a few guesses about what he meant but they were neither killers nor torturers. But still I was worried about both of them. Yes. I got worried about Ben, too. He might've not been there for me for the past year but he had always been there for me. I can't forget like eighteen years for one year! He's my brother. We're the same blood.

"Yeah! That doesn't sound like him at all," Charlotte said.

I was kind of shocked how good she knew James. I haven't seen many girls who knew James this well. Actually, I haven't seen any girl who knew him. He was a player and still is. But it seemed like Charlotte kind of liked him. I don't know. Maybe it was because of all the hormones and stuff.

"I agree. It doesn't sound like any of them," I said.

Charles flipped the pancakes before I'd burn them. I was pretty deep in my thoughts. I had left my phone upstairs so I could avoid my dad's calls easier.

"I hope they don't do anything stupid," Charles said.

He might have just said it but I really hoped it. I knew them and I knew my dad, too. He was capable of doing anything. And when I say anything, I mean anything, even killing.

"I don't think James would do anything stupid," Charlotte said, defending James.

I was just wishing for the best. We talked till the pancakes were ready and Mister Young came back. We kept talking about different things and fortunately it kept my mind off of James and Ben and what they might do.

After breakfast we changed into warmer clothes and went

for a walk in the snow. It was freezing out there. We ended up building a snowman in the back yard. It was pretty big and beautiful.

I learned a lot about Charlotte and Christian. Charlotte was a senior this year and hoped to join NYU next year to study drama. Christian unlike Charles and Charlotte was not interested in art or at least not interested enough to study any kind of art. He was studying civil engineering at NYU. Apparently, it was kind of a tradition for them to go to NYU since both their parents went to NYU and met there.

The day passed by pretty fast and pretty nice. They were the nicest people I have ever met. When we went back inside, we ate a little something for lunch since we were mostly full from the late breakfast and then Charlotte brought some old photo albums. They were so adorable. Charles and Christian looked a lot like each other when they were younger. It was hard to tell which one was Charles and which one was Christian. They still look a lot like each other but you can tell which one is which now.

Charles has darker hair and Christian has a rounder face. Charles looks somehow older than Christian even though they're twins. I don't know. Maybe it's just the way I see them is different.

Mister Young didn't let us in the kitchen as he was cooking dinner. Charles said it was his parents' thing. They always cooked Christmas dinner together and for the last few years his dad did it all by himself. It was so sweet.

This was the perfect family. Not because they are rich but because they are there for each other. It used to make my heart ache to face how alone I was. But now I feel like I belong somewhere even if it's for a short period of time.

I didn't know what it was that he cooked but it was so delicious. We helped in cleaning up the kitchen since he was pretty tired. Then we grabbed our wine glasses and went back to the living room. Charlotte had just turned eighteen a few weeks ago and it was her first Christmas drinking with her family.

I got my phone after dinner because Charlotte asked to see some of my paintings. My dad called a few times but I didn't pick up, he didn't leave a single message either. It was getting pretty late and I was tired. He called again and I send him straight to voicemail again. He left a message this time. He left a pretty long one. Then he texted me a link and wrote 'I'm so sorry for everything I didn't do before. I got your justice'. I was shocked.

I excused myself and grabbed my coat and walked out. I was standing on the porch, staring at my phone. After a few minutes, I pressed play. I needed to know what he wanted to tell me. I could feel it was important.

"Hi Brooke! It's your dad. I know. You don't want to talk to me. I don't blame you. I haven't been a good father. I haven't been even a dad. I'm sorry Brooke. I know it doesn't matter how many times I say it, it won't do anything. I wish I listened to you that day. I wish I knew you a little more to notice there was something serious going on with you. Brooke, I noticed you were sleeping in the living room but I was too much of an asshole to ask you what was going on with you. Brooke, I know I couldn't get justice for you legally now. And I am so sorry about it. I needed to do things a little differently. I didn't listen to you back then but now I am listening. You deserved a proper justice and I hope it's enough. Brooke? Baby girl, I am so sorry for letting you down time after time.

I had to be there for you. I should have been there for you. I hope you let me be there for you from now on. You have no idea how proud of you I am. You're not just an eighteen years old girl. You became an independent woman who can take care of herself. You know, your paintings are hanging in my office. I look at them every day. I really missed you. I hope I can see you someday. I love you," he said.

I couldn't help my tears. They dropped down my face one after the other. I took a few deep breaths before opening the link he sent me earlier. The headline said 'Max Murray, Jack Murray's younger son was found dead.'

I felt my heart dropped in my chest. He was dead? Did my dad do that? Was this the thing James and Ben wanted to take care of. I felt a strong pain in my chest. I tried to breathe deeply but it didn't do a damn thing. My head was spinning around. I could hardly breathe any more. I blinked a few times but I couldn't see less blurry. I wanted to go back inside but as I took my first step, I fell and within a few second everything went black.

Chapter Fifteen

It's been a while since Brooke went outside. It was freezing out there. She grabbed her coat but she wouldn't be so warm with that to keep her outside for more than half an hour. I decided to go check on her. I got up to go check on her. After I took a few steps, my phone rang. It was James.

"Hey! Merry Christmas! How are you?" I said as I picked up.

"Charles? Tell me Brooke is with you," he said.

I could say he was pretty worried. It was so sudden. I got worried, too.

"No, she's not with me right now. She went outside. She must be on the porch," I said.

"Go check on her now," he said even more anxiously.

"James? Is everything all right?" I asked as I was going to check on Brooke.

"She might've heard some news and we're not sure if she can handle it right now. Just tell me she's fine," he said.

"Okay!" I said.

A few seconds later, as I opened the door, I saw her passed out on the porch. I gasped. James heard it.

"Charles? What's happening there?" he asked.

"She's passed out. I got to go," I said and hung up.

I didn't even let him say another word. I just shoved my phone into my pocket and lifted her on my arms and took her inside. Her body was ice cold. Her heartbeat was slow but it was steady. I put her on the couch since the living room was warmer than my room. My dad has gone to bed but fortunately Charlotte and Christian were still there.

"What happened?" Charlotte asked shocked.

"I have no idea," I said.

"Should I call nine-one-one?" Christian asked.

"It takes them too long to get here! Can she breathe?" she asked.

"Yeah," I checked and said.

I was shaking so much. I couldn't think straight. I was sitting beside her, didn't know what to do. I was too scared. I couldn't even check her pulse.

"Charles?" Charlotte said and tried to pull me out of my head.

"Charles! She can't breathe properly." Christian said and I jumped.

Charlotte sat by her and tried to open her mouth so she could breath. None of us had any idea how to wake her up. It was getting more and more scary by the second. Christian ran to the kitchen and came back with a glass of water. He splashed some water on her face. I had no idea what he was doing. But it was helping. She could breathe properly after Charlotte opened her mouth. After a few minutes of splashing water on her face, she woke up.

As she opened her eyes, I pulled her in my arms and held her tight. I was scared something would happen to her. She was still shocked.

"What happened?" she asked as she pulled away.

"You passed out on the porch," I said.

Fortunately, she remembered all of us. But she was still in

shock for something I didn't know. After a few minutes I texted James to tell him she woke up. There was something that I didn't know and it was affecting Brooke so much.

Charlotte and Christian went to bed after they made sure we were all right. I felt like I would pass out any second. We stayed in the living room, cuddling for a little while since she shouldn't have slept right away after she woke up. I couldn't quite read her eyes which I usually can. There was a mixed look of pain and happiness in her eyes.

"Brooke? What happened?" I asked after a while we were alone.

"Someone I knew died," she said.

But there was no emotion in her voice which was odd. She was the most emotional person I've ever known. She might not show it much but when she talks about something like someone's death, you can hear how sad she is. Her voice was so numb like she was talking about someone she didn't know or even someone she hated which I think is impossible.

"Can we sleep here?" she asked after a few minutes.

"Why?" I asked with curiosity.

"I'm too tired to walk to your room," she said and put her head on my chest.

I got up. She was confused at first but when I lifted her up on my arms, she started to laugh. She covered her mouth so she wouldn't wake anyone up.

"Comfortable?" I asked as I put her on the bed and covered her with a warm blanket.

"Thanks!" she said with a cute smile on her face.

"But I got to run to the bathroom," she said and got up.

As she was in the bathroom, I checked my phone. James had text me back.

"Please look out for her." He wrote.

I was confused. She got the news that someone she knew died and she passed out. But she talked about it with no emotion and now James is talking like she loved this person so much.

"James, who died? She's acting weird." I texted back.

"Someone who wasn't nice to her." He replied.

But it wouldn't explain anything. Was this person a girl or a guy? Why weren't they nice to her? How does James know about it and I don't? I kept asking so many questions in my head but there was no answer to any of them.

"Okay! We'll talk later." I texted back.

She took a pill and we went to bed but I couldn't sleep. Brooke fell asleep immediately in my arms. Her head was buried in my chest. I was playing with her hair but she was too tired to wake up from it. I couldn't stop thinking about what happened tonight. About how she passed out on the porch and I wasn't there to catch her. About how she was clearly hiding something from me. About how James called me. It was so confusing but at the same time it felt like they were hiding something from me.

It took me hours to fall asleep but I couldn't sleep much. I woke up around seven in the morning. I couldn't stay in bed for long. I got up and took a shower. Brooke was still sound asleep. I got dressed and went downstairs to make some coffee. I already had a headache from lack of sleep.

"You're up early!" Christian said as he walked in the kitchen.

"I couldn't sleep," I said.

"How's she?" he asked.

"Still asleep," I said and poured some coffee for both of

us.

"How are you? You looked pretty scared last night," He asked.

"I don't know how I am. I couldn't sleep much last night. I couldn't get this out of my head that she's hiding something from me. Neither Brooke nor James says what's going on," I said.

"How's James involved with this?" he asked.

"Honestly I don't even know! He just said he called me to see if Brooke's with me at the time. He sounded pretty worried. I really didn't think about it at the time but now I don't even know what happened. She said someone she knew died. Oh, I feel like I don't know anything," I said and sighed.

"Give her some time. She's known you for like ten days. You can't expect her to tell you every single detail of her life or past. You know her but she doesn't really know you," he said.

"You're right. I've known her for like two years now but she had no idea I even existed till ten days ago. I should give her some time," I said.

But as much as I wanted to be that guy and give her time, I couldn't stop thinking she was hiding something from me. And I knew whatever it was, that was the reason she passed out on the porch last night. I wasn't just curious. I was worried about her.

"How are you doing? We haven't really talked in a while," I said, to change the subject.

"The usual. Classes and stuff," he said.

"I thought you'd be here with someone this year," I said.

"I'm not as lucky as you are," he said and laughed.

Well, I've been single for like a year. And ever since I saw

Brooke in the hallway, I couldn't go out with any other girl. It was just not fun anymore. I preferred to stay home and work.

"Yeah! I'm pretty lucky," I said with a smile.

"I hope I get this lucky one day," he said.

Charlotte and Brooke came downstairs after a while. My dad came a little later. He must have been working. He would never sleep after eight, not even in the holidays. He'd wake up automatically.

Brooke was better this morning. There was no sign of pain or anything in her eyes or the way she talked. It was pretty weird for me. We spent our morning mostly in the kitchen and in the back yard, throwing snow balls at each other. Our snowman was still in perfect shape. It was still snowing. I was worried that the road would get blocked.

After lunch, me and Brooke went to my bedroom to take a nap. We were both pretty tired but before we could even lie down, James called.

"Hi! How's everything?" he said as I picked up.

"Good. How are you?" I asked.

"Is there a better word than perfect?" he asked happily.

"What's going on?" I asked with laughter.

"Is Brooke there?" he asked.

"Yeah!" I said confused.

"Put me on speaker phone. I'll tell you," he said.

"Hey James!" Brooke said as I put him on speaker.

"Hi! So, guys do you remember we got a bunch of emails for interviews that we totally forgot about?" he said excited.

"Yeah!" she said.

"Well, a bunch of them emailed me again and asked if they could talk to us this week! They probably emailed you two as well. So, I did a little digging and picked a few of them and told them they can interview us this week," he said.

"Well, that's amazing," I said.

"But when is the first interview?" she asked.

"It's on Monday afternoon," he said.

"It's the day after tomorrow!" I said.

"Yeah! I thought you'd come back tomorrow!" he said.

"Yeah, we will. Are you okay with this?" I askcd Brooke.

"Yeah!" she said.

"Okay. So, we'll see you tomorrow," I said.

"See you," he said and hung up.

"Are you really okay with this? I mean after the robbery and all of this, do you think it's a good idea to do this?" I asked.

"Yeah! The sooner we do this, the better we can do it," she said.

We went to bed to took a nap. She fell asleep pretty fast. I could get some sleep, too. But I woke up with her body shaking in my arms. As I opened my eyes, I saw her face covered in tears. She wasn't crying out loud or shouting or screaming. The tears were streaming down her face with no sound.

I didn't know if I should've woken her up or not. I waited for a few minutes but it didn't stop. It just got worse. I woke her up. It took a few minutes. As she opened her eyes, she jumped into my arms and held me as tight as she could. I was shocked at first but then I wrapped my arms around her and kissed her head.

Chapter Sixteen

As he was holding me down by my waist, he thrusted me time after time, harder and harder. He kept on going till I came but he didn't stop. He was still going. My body couldn't take it anymore and I just passed out under him.

As I opened my eyes and saw Charles, I jumped into his arms and held him with all my strength. It took him a few seconds to wrap his arms around me. He kissed my head as I was in his arms. My face was covered in tears. My body was covered in sweat. My heart was beating so fast, it could pop out of my chest any second.

"Brooke? What's wrong? What's happening?" he asked.

I couldn't hold back anymore. I just started to cry in his arms.

"My nightmares, they're back," I said after a few minutes.

I didn't lie to him. I've been having nightmares for months. I only had a peaceful sleep for a few nights. I'd wake up like this for months and the medications didn't help much. It was the third time I slept since I got my memories back. And it was the only time I didn't take any pills. Maybe I just need to start taking them again.

"I'm sorry baby," he said and kissed my head again.

He held me for a while before I got up and went to the bathroom. I really needed to take a shower. I could still feel his filthy hands on my body. His hands were not the only things I still could feel. I could feel the pain in my whole body. I could still see the bruises.

After I got out of the shower, I just blow dried my hair and got dressed. I buried myself in the covers and tried to keep myself warm. I took another pill before I got back to bed. It wouldn't help me sleep. It would just keep my heartbeat steady.

Charles wasn't in the room so I thought it would be a good time to find out what happened to that son of a bitch. I grabbed my phone and check out the link my dad sent me last night. I didn't know if I was ready or not but I thought the sooner I find out, the easier it'll be.

It was a pretty short article for such a powerful family in New York. It just said he was found with a bullet in his head in his car in the middle of the woods.

A bullet in his head? My heart ached for some reason. I couldn't believe it. My dad really killed him. My dad killed my rapist. He killed his best friend's son. But the bullet didn't heal me. It just twisted the knife in my heart somehow. Did I really think I could face him again? Or I rather him dead? Could he even face me again?

I finished school from home last year so I didn't see him after that fucking night. But no, I couldn't see his evil eyes. I couldn't shake the hands that caused me so much pain. Or would I really see him again? I knew I wouldn't go to my parents' New Year's Eve party anyway.

I couldn't take it anymore. I just put my phone on the nightstand, took another pill and tried to sleep. I could sleep for a few hours. Fortunately, I didn't have any nightmares. Charles woke me up for dinner. I went downstairs to have dinner with them but I really couldn't eat much. Charles and I stayed up a little longer than them. We were cuddling in front of the fire place. Charles was playing with my hair and it kept my mind off of everything for a while.

"Brooke? Have you ever lied to me?" he asked out of nowhere.

"Why would you ask that?" I asked freaked out.

I hoped James didn't tell him anything. But if he did, Charles wouldn't act so calm and normal.

"Have you?" he asked again.

He looked pretty serious. And I didn't know how to answer it. Would it count as lying that I didn't tell him I got my memories back? It wouldn't really.

"I haven't," I said.

"But if, if I lie to you someday, know that it was just for your own sake," I said after a few minutes of silence.

I really felt guilty. He had no idea what was going on in my head. We weren't together for long but it felt more like ten months than ten days. I could say he was really worried about me but I couldn't drag him into this mess with myself. I couldn't mess up his mind.

"Please don't! I don't know what you're keeping from me now. Maybe you're just not ready to talk about it. But I want to know you better, no matter what," he said.

I turned in his arms to face him. He was looking at me like nothing could make him run away from me, like there was nothing else important in the world. But still, I couldn't say one word.

"I know you might not trust me yet. But I really want to know you more and I want you to know me better, too," He was practically begging me to trust him.

But he didn't know I already trusted him with all of my

heart and soul. He was something especial. I thought I could never trust anyone ever again. I was working on my trust issues so much when I was with Nick but he did something that just made my trust issues even worse. But I trusted Charles. I wasn't sure why I trusted him so much. Was it because James trusted him? It could be the reason.

I brushed his hair out of his face and pulled him closer and kissed him. He smiled on my lips but I could feel it wasn't a happy smile.

"You already know me perfectly. But Charles, I need to figure this on my own first," I said as my hand was still on his face.

He smiled sadly but didn't say anything else. I really wanted to tell him but I was too scared to say a word. I was with the best guy on the planet. I couldn't afford to lose him. I was feeling things with Charles that I have never felt before with anyone. I couldn't scare him away.

We stayed there for a little longer. When we went back to his room, I took another pill before we went to bed. He was looking at me with the most anxious look I could ever see in anyone's eyes. But he didn't say anything. We went to bed and I fell asleep pretty fast because of the pill I took.

The next morning, I woke up pretty early. I went downstairs to make something for breakfast. As I went to the kitchen, I saw Charlotte there. She was already making the batter for waffles.

"Good morning!" I said as I went closer.

"Good morning! How did you sleep?" she asked.

"Pretty good! How did you sleep? You went to bed pretty early last night," I said.

"Yeah! It was good," she said with a huge smile on her

face.

"Good like you were talking to a guy till four in the morning or like you sneaked in a guy?" I asked with a smirk.

"I was talking to someone. How did you know?" she asked.

She was blushing so much. Aww! She was so sweet. And I felt like she was talking to James last night. I didn't even know why I felt that way.

"We're like the same age. I know what girls my age do," I said with a smile.

She blushed even more.

"So, tell me about this lucky guy," I said with curiosity.

"Can you keep a secret?" she asked in a low voice.

I nodded and waited for her answer. She took a deep breath before saying anything.

"I've been talking to James for a while now but nobody knows," she said.

"A while?" I asked in shock.

It couldn't be right. He was hitting on a drunk girl last week and went out with another girl the night of my exhibition. How can this be possible? He's a total player. Didn't she know? It wasn't making any sense! James could be playing her but no. He wouldn't do that to his best friend's little sister.

"Yeah!" she said.

I couldn't understand. Did she really think he was boyfriend material? I couldn't say a word in minutes. Every time I opened my mouth to say something, words would get lost.

"Brooke? Is everything all right?" she asked.

"Charlotte? How much do you know James?" I asked, too

scared to hear the answer.

"Pretty well. Why?" she said.

I couldn't say anything else. How could she be serious? He's a good friend but he was not a good boyfriend. He was a player.

"Is this about him being a player?" she asked like it was no big deal.

"Yeah!" I said.

She just laughed. I couldn't get it. She seemed like a pretty smart girl. How couldn't she not care? Didn't she care? Really?

"Charlotte, I love James so much. He's like a brother to me but he's not boyfriend material," I said.

I really didn't want her to get hurt especially by James. He broke many hearts before.

"Yeah! I would agree with you a few months ago. But not now," she said with a huge smile on her lips.

I had to tell her what I saw in the last two weeks.

"Charlotte, I've seen him hitting on a drunk girl in a coffee house at eight in the morning. He left my exhibition with another girl. Please don't get me wrong. I just don't want you to get hurt especially by him! He broke too many hearts," I said.

I couldn't help it. I was worried sick about her. She didn't know what she was getting herself into. She just smiled.

"Brooke, nobody knows about us. So, if he stopped messing around so suddenly, Charles would be the first one to figure it out. And when Charles asks me something I can't lie. I can't even hide something from him. So, we decided to keep it down. I knew if Charles or Christian found out about us it would get ruined and none of us wanted that," she said.

I was shocked. I couldn't believe it. James was able to do

this? Wait! Did he tell her about me or that son of a bitch? I hoped not.

"And we thought if we broke up badly one day, it might ruin his friendship with Charles and Christian. But I can say he's changed so much in the past two years," she said with a huge smile on her lips.

"But what about last week? I saw him walk out of my exhibition with a girl," I asked because I was still confused.

"Yeah! He needed to make an excuse for stay out late. He was with me that night," she said.

Wow! I couldn't believe it. James, the one who everyone knows as a player has a girlfriend. And she was my boyfriend's sister. Okay! It might get complicated. He knew my secret and Charles didn't. Was it possible that he told her anything?

"Wow! I can't believe he did all this to keep it from Charles and even me," I said after a few minutes of silence.

She was smiling like nothing could ever take away her happiness. She was making the waffles and I made some coffee.

"Are you planning to tell your brothers?" I asked after a while.

"Yeah! I mean I should tell them eventually. But I can't tell them now. They'll kill him before I get the chance to explain that it was just in act," she said.

"Fair enough. If he was here, even I would hit him," I said with a little laughter.

Christian was the first one to join us. Charles and his dad came a little later. We had breakfast and cleaned up together. We were going back to the city today. We were scared the roads might get blocked because of the snow. We packed up and hit the roads a little after noon.

Chapter Seventeen

I woke up with the worst headache ever. I took a pretty heavy painkiller last night before I slept, why do I have this headache? I must have had bad dreams again. I can't remember now but it's possible. I gathered all my straight and got out of my bed. I really needed a hot shower and a cup of coffee to get rid of my headache.

I took a hot steamy shower as soon as I could get out the bed. I blow dried my hair before my headache could get any worse. I had to straighten it later but for now it was enough. I made some coffee, toasts and eggs. It was nearly noon so I ate enough to skip lunch. I wasn't in the mood to eat at all. I really lost my appetite in the past few days.

After I ate, I cleaned up a little and went back to my room. I straightened my hair and put on a little makeup. I wasn't sure what I should've worn. But since it was snowing outside and I was already freezing, I decided to wear something that I wouldn't freeze in.

I wore a pair of blue jeans, a knitted rainbow sweater, a pair of burgundy knee height boots with a puffy white waterproof coat. I grabbed a little white leather backpack and put my stuff in it. It was still a little early but I wanted to talk to James. So, I called him to see if he was home alone.

"Hi!" he said as he picked up.

"Hey. James? Are you alone?" I asked.

"Yeah! Is everything okay?" he asked.

"Yeah, I just need to talk to you about something," I said.

"Okay! Come over," he said.

I got out of the apartment within a few minutes. I got a cab. It wasn't that far but I wouldn't walk there in this weather. I would freeze.

I didn't know if I should ask him about Charlotte first or about what they did to that son of a bitch. But I knew I had to talk about both of them. I'm not sorry for him but I needed to know who killed him. But at the same time, I was scared that Ben or James had pulled the trigger.

I didn't get much time to torture myself over it. I was at their place within ten minutes. Before I knocked, I took a deep breath. It took him a few seconds to open the door. He was all dressed up for the interview.

"Hey! Come on in," he said as he opened the door.

"James, we need to talk," I said seriously.

"Okay! Is this about that bastard?" he asked as he took my coat.

"Yes! What have you done?" I asked seriously.

I was going to ask him about Charlotte first but that could wait. I couldn't wait for this. I had to know.

"I did nothing nor did Ben. We just dug up a little information about him. Your dad did most of the work," he said.

"So, you led my dad to him?" I said.

"Yeah something like that," he said.

"Who killed him? Who pulled the trigger?" I asked seriously.

There was no emotion in my voice. I was kind of scared of myself right now. But why would I even show any kind of emotion for that monster? How could I have any emotion for that pervert?

"Your dad. We told him to stay out of this and let one of his guys do this but he wouldn't listen. He said he needed to get your justice himself," he said.

Justice? He wanted justice for me? So, then who would get my justice from my dad? Did he really think he had fixed everything when he killed that fucking asshole?

I couldn't say a word for a few minutes. I needed to calm down. I was too furious at my dad. I sat on the couch and put my head on my hands. I closed my eyes for a few minutes. I wasn't in a good place. I didn't know what to do or what to feel. I just wanted to let go and move on.

"Brooke? Are you okay?" he asked as he sat by my side.

"Hell no! My dad has killed someone with his own hands. He killed his best friend's son who I was supposed to marry one day. I'm not sad that he died. But I'm not happy either. I don't know if it did me any good or maybe it did. I don't know! It just hurts James. It hurts a lot," I said and tried to hold back my tears.

"You were supposed to what?" he asked in shock, with rage.

"Yeah! Our families wanted us to get married," I said as I leaned back on the couch.

He got up with rage. He went straight to the kitchen and grabbed a beer. He drank it pretty quickly. He tossed the empty bottle in the trash can and took another one. He drank that pretty fast, too. He was about to get his third one. So, I got up and took the bottle from his hand.

"It's enough," I said seriously.

"Is it though?" he asked.

I could say he was upset but I didn't know why exactly. Because there were many reasons to be upset right now.

"Yes! We have an interview in less than an hour and I'm not planning to tell Charles today. So, get your shit together," I said with a straight face.

It was driving me crazy. I was having all of this mixed feelings and rage and I didn't know what to do with them.

He went to the living room and laid on the couch. I put the beer back in the fridge and threw away the empty bottle he left on the counter. I grabbed a glass and filled it with ice and then poured water on it. I hoped it could calm him down a little.

As I went back to the living room, I gave him the glass and sat on the opposite end of the couch. He drank some of the water and cooled down a little.

"James, there's something else I need to talk to you about. It's about Charlotte," I said.

"What about her?" He sat up quickly as he said.

"Didn't she tell you anything?" I asked confused.

"She told me you know. Is there something else?" he asked.

He was still looking pretty worried.

"No. Just relax. I just wanted to talk to you about her," I said.

He was looking at me all confused and worried.

"How serious are you? I mean you've never been in a relationship before. You were always messing round," I said.

"I don't really know. I mean I know I was always sleeping around and I don't have any kind of good reputation, but I really like her. And I was pretty scared at first to ask her out. But it's been a nice few months," he said.

"So why are still acting like before? Do you want to keep it a secret forever?" I asked.

"I don't know. I mean both of us are scared of Christian and Charles. We don't know how they would react," he said.

"So, stop messing around. If you keep acting like before they would never believe you actually changed!" I said.

"Do you really think that would work?" he asked.

"It's still worth a shot. I mean if you keep messing around even in act, you might never get a chance to prove you have actually changed," I said.

"Okay!" he said.

He got up and called Charlotte. Apparently, they had plans for tonight. He apologized that he canceled on her but then he explained what he was doing. They were on the phone for a while. He hung up just a few minutes before Charles arrived.

"Hey!" he said as he came in.

"Hi!" I said with a smile.

He gave me a kiss before going to his room and changing into something more comfortable than the clothes he was wearing.

"Are you nervous?" he asked as he came back.

"No, not really," I said.

"Good, because I'm freaking out!" he said.

He was pretty nervous. He went to the kitchen and I followed him. I put my hands on his face and kissed him.

"There's nothing to be nervous about. Okay? Just avoid unrelated questions," I said.

He just smiled weakly in return.

The journalist was there at five. The interview took about an hour or so. I was trying my best to avoid the questions about Nick and Bella but it was somehow impossible. So, I just answered shortly. I wanted to stay out of the interview as much as possible. I wanted her to talk to Charles and James more, even though she was somehow flirting with Charles and it bothered me a lot.

As she left, I let out a deep breath with a sigh. I took off my boots and sat back on the couch. James laughed a little at my sigh.

"What?" I asked.

"You literally couldn't be more annoyed," James said.

"She was lucky I didn't kick her out," I said and rolled my eyes.

"Why?" Charles asked confused.

My eyes widened. Why? Didn't he notice she was flirting with him? Or did he enjoy it?

"Oh, come on! She was all over you," James said.

"Oh!" he said.

"Charles! She's going to kick your ass if you…" James was saying when I cut him off.

"James! Stop! I'm not going to kick anybody's ass." I said weakly.

I was kind of tired and sleepy. It was only seven and I already wanted to go back home and sleep. I couldn't keep my eyes open for longer than thirty seconds.

"Brooke? Are you okay?" Charles asked.

"Yeah! I'm just tired, I guess," I said.

I closed my eyes for a few seconds. I was falling asleep. Charles sat by me and wrapped his arm around my shoulders. I rested my head on his shoulder but I opened my eyes before I'd fall asleep.

"I think I'd better go home," I said as I pulled out of his arm.

"Are you sure you're just tired?" Charles asked as I was putting on my boots.

"Yeah!" I said and gave him a kiss.

He got his keys and coat and we left. I kept myself busy during the ride so I wouldn't fall asleep. I played with my hair or drew on the window. I just wanted to stay awake till we get there. As we got to my place, I kissed him goodbye and went up to my apartment.

I could barely keep my eyes open. I just put on some comfortable clothes and removed my makeup. As soon as I laid down, I fell asleep.

Chapter Eighteen

The past two days have been mostly the same and yet different. It was tiring and exhausting but not as painful. I could let loose a little with the help of a little cocaine. Yes, cocaine. My thoughts were killing me and I was screwing up the interviews.

On Tuesday, we had three interviews and I kind of screwed up the first one. I couldn't focus at all. So, I called someone I knew back in high school whom I knew could get me any kind of drugs. I told him I needed to let loose and he suggested coke. I made up an excuse to get out the guys' apartment to get the coke from him. It finally made me calm when nothing could help me.

I'm not planning to take it for a long time. Maybe just for a few weeks till I find a way to finally move on with my life and leave this whole thing behind me.

I called my therapist yesterday. She was so happy when I told her that I could finally get my memories back but as I told her what I remembered, she asked me to see her. I went to her house since the clinic was closed. We talked for a while. I told her how I can't sleep at night. I couldn't tell her about the cocaine. Maybe I was ashamed, maybe I needed it for now. I don't know.

She gave me a prescription for a few medications to help me sleep at night. She told me not to take them with any kind of drugs or alcoholic drinks. I didn't know if she knew I was still a little high when I went to see her or not. But somehow, I think she knew.

Today I woke around noon. The pill I took every night was strong enough to keep me asleep for more than ten hours. I was not in the mood to do anything so I just ordered some food and stayed in bed till it arrived. I ate my breakfast/lunch and took a bath. Charles was going to pick me up at six so I had plenty of time to get ready. It was New Year's Eve.

I did my hair a little different. I curled it and then brushed it out to make waves. I wore a satin red maxi dress with a slit, long enough to show all my leg. I paired it with a pair of crimson red high heels and a pair of diamond earrings. I put on a full glam makeup with my favorite dark red lipstick. I took some coke before Charles would pick me up. I packed a little incase I needed some in the party.

"Wow!" he said as I opened the door.

"You can't even see me dress," I said since I was already wearing my cape.

"Yeah! But I know you look amazing and I can't say a wow like this in front of others," he said and kissed me.

As his lips touched mine, my heart ached. He didn't know what he was getting himself into by dating me and I was too much of a coward to tell him.

"Can I ruin you makeup?" he asked as he pulled away.

"In a few hours, yes!" I said with a smirk.

He smirked and held out his arm for me to take it.

"So, let's kill these few hours faster," he said as I grabbed his arm.

I just smiled and didn't say anything. I locked up and we went to his parents' penthouse uptown. We were the first ones to arrive. James came a little later. He was pretty cute with

Charlotte. They tried to keep it normal but the smiles on their faces would say everything but nobody saw it since Charles couldn't get his eyes off of me and Christian was busy with his new girlfriend.

The party was like any other rich people's party. There were live music and Charles played a few songs, too. He asked me if I'd play with him but I said I wasn't sober enough to play. I didn't lie. I was high on the coke and I had two glasses of wine. Even if I didn't take the coke, I wouldn't be able to play.

The night was going well but when my family walked in, I felt my heart stopped for a second. Why were they here? Who invited them? But before I could ask Charles anything, I saw his dad welcoming my family. Wow! That was the only thing I needed tonight.

"Brooke? Is everything all right?" Charles asked after a few minutes that I was staring at them.

"Charles? Why is my family here?" I asked upset.

"I don't know! My dad must have invited them," he said.

"Wait. Your dad knows my family?" I asked.

"I think so! I mean they do a lot of business together," he said.

I felt a heavy dizziness in my head. I just grabbed his arm to keep myself from falling. He helped me to sit down and left me for a few minutes to grab me something that hopefully could make me feel better. Before Charles came back, Ben and James came to me.

"What the hell are you doing here?" I asked Ben.

"Josh invited us and dad thought he could see you," Ben said.

"Oh, Josh? What the fuck were you thinking? That I

would talk to him ever again?" I stood up and as I asked.

"Brooke, he deserved it," James said.

"No James! I deserved to be heard but he took that away from me when he walked out on me. What is he even trying to prove? That he's a good father? Well, tell him he's not," I said.

"Brooke, you got to give him a chance. He's sorry," Ben said.

"Ben, the only reason I am talking to you right now is because I saw how sorry you were that you didn't come home for my birthday and you think what happened to me wouldn't happen if you were there. But what would be the reason to talk to the man who never gave a shit about me my whole life? Did he even tell mom that I got my memories back? Does she know what I remember?" I said and tried to keep calm.

I wished I could scream at them but I couldn't. I wish I could hit him as hard as I could but I couldn't, not here.

"He thought it's better if you tell her yourself." Ben said in a low voice that I could barely hear.

"Tell him he better forgets he ever had a daughter," I said and walked away.

I found Charles talking to someone I didn't know so I didn't get close. I went to the bathroom and locked myself there to get away from the crowd. I couldn't take it anymore. I did the only thing I thought I could do. I took some more coke. It was a few hours since I took some. I could handle some more now. I took it and it burned my nose and throat instantly. I sat there till the burning got better.

It was nearly midnight. I just wanted to leave as soon as possible. I found Charles wondering around, looking for me with a glass of water in his hand.

"Where were you? I looked everywhere for you." He

asked worried.

"I was in the bathroom," I said with a smile like nothing has happened.

He was looking at me anxiously. He was looking at me this way since I passed out on that porch. He was somehow right to be worried. That was actually why I didn't tell him about the coke and Max. He had the right to know what's going on with me. But I couldn't admit it. Not to him anyway. I was too afraid to lose him when I just found him.

It was getting closer and closer to midnight and I couldn't wait to get out of there. I wanted to talk to Charlotte tonight about her situation with James but I didn't know if it was a good idea or not. As soon as I found her alone, I went to her.

"Charlotte? Can we talk for a minute?" I asked.

"Sure!" she said with her beautiful smile.

"Are you planning on telling your brothers about, umm, you know, your relationship?" I asked.

I was kind of worried she might get angry at me. But fortunately, she didn't. She knew how much I loved James. Besides Charlotte and I were getting closer. I really wanted them both to be happy.

"Actually, I thought tonight might be a good time to tell them since they're both drunk! I was wondering if you could be there too when I tell them?" she said with a smile.

"Sure," I said with a smile and pulled her in my arms.

She went to grab Christian and James and I went to find Charles. We went to her room so she could tell them what's going on.

"What are we doing here?" Christian asked confused.

I think no one really noticed how Charlotte smiles when anyone talks about James or even just say his name. James was holding her hand. It made Christian and Charles even more confused.

"Well, I wanted to let you know that we're dating," she said.

She was scared a little for sure. James couldn't breathe. I was fine. Charles and Christian were shocked and couldn't say a single word. After a few minutes they realized I wasn't shocked at all. I was the only one there who was calm. I didn't know whether it was because of the coke or the fact that I already knew. Whatever it was, it felt so good not be scared. I felt like a God!

"Wait! Did you know about them?" Charles asked confused.

"Well, yeah! It was pretty obvious Charlotte likes James. She didn't even try to hide it in front of you guys," I said.

"How long has this been going on?" Christian asked, trying to put all the pieces together.

"It's been a few months," James answered.

Charlotte was a little scared to talk. I didn't blame her. I was like her before the accident.

"Remember if you hurt her, I'll kill you!" Charles said, pointing at James.

"Was I supposed to tell you the same thing when you two started dating?" James asked.

"Well, yeah! You're a little late but I'm not," Charles said seriously.

"I promise I won't hurt her," James said.

"And I promise I won't hurt Brooke," Charles said.

"Should I promise anything or can I go kiss my girlfriend at midnight?" Christian asked.

It was less than ten minutes till midnight. All of us were

with the one we loved, side by side. We counted down to midnight and kissed on the stroke of midnight.

"Can we leave?" I whispered in his ear.

It was almost one. We've had stayed enough. I wanted to go home.

"Sure," he said with a smirk.

We left there as soon as we could. We took a cab to my apartment since both of us were absolutely drunk. As soon as we stepped in my apartment, I closed the door and pushed him against it. My hands were on his chest keeping him on the door. I kept him waiting for a few seconds in silence.

I slid my hands to his neck and hair and pulled him closer slowly. His hands were on my waist, putting a little pressure on it. I kept one hand in his hair and slid the other one to his face. My fingers brushed against his lips. I went closer and kissed him. As soon as my lips touched his, he pulled me toward himself, pressing my body against his.

His hands slid to my butt and pressed me to himself. I pressed myself to him even more. I could feel him getting hard under me. I bit his bottom lip and pulled it a little. We were both still fully dressed. I was the first one to take anything off. I took off his overcoat and coat at the same time and threw it on the ground. He slowly slid his hands under my cape and took it off. He knew how to tease me and I liked it.

As soon as my cape was on the ground, he grabbed my thighs and lifted me up. He took me to my bedroom and put me on my bed. He took off his tie and shirt quickly. He came to me and laid me on my bed. He kissed my neck down to my chest. He was searching for my dress's zipper with his hand at the same time. As he found it, he pulled it down slowly. I got up and took off my dress. I was left in my panties and my heels.

I took off his pants as I was still standing. Before I could think of my next move, I was on the bed with Charles on top of me. He was kissing me passionately. He was keeping his weight with one hand by my head and his other hand was on my thigh. He didn't have much finger nails but they were in my thigh, causing a pleasing pain. It was nothing compare to how my nails were scratching his back.

I didn't know if he knew it or not but I was completely wet. I tried to press my thighs together to decrease the pain between them. I moaned in his mouth subconsciously. I was shaking under his touch again. I couldn't keep going like that. I didn't know whether it was because of the alcohol or the coke or Charles himself but I knew I needed him.

I slid my hands to his boxers and tried to take them off but I couldn't. He kissed me down to my chest again and kissed my breasts. I threw my head back in pleasure but I needed more. He took off my panties slowly and then he took off his boxers. He was pretty hard. He put on a condom quickly and came back on top of me.

He kissed me a few times before entering me. I moaned loudly in pain and pleasure. I wrapped my legs around his hips and pulled him as close as I possibly could. With each move he made; he'd go deeper. Pain and pleasure filled my body.

"Charles!" I called out his name loudly.

It made him go faster. As he was moving back and forth, I moaned more. I tightened my legs around his hips. I was so close. My whole body was shaking under him. I couldn't stay still. I moaned as I came. He came a few seconds after me. If he went for a little longer, I would easily come again.

As he pulled out, he went down between my thighs and

licked me up and then kissed me. I was already turned on again but I knew my body couldn't take more than this. Charles lay next to me and pulled me in his arms. His arm was wrapped around my shoulders and my head was on his chest. As his legs were parted, I slipped my leg between them to get closer to him.

"Happy New Year!" he said.

"Happy New Year!" I said and kissed him.

Chapter Nineteen

As I opened my eyes, I found myself in my old bedroom. I was still naked and my whole body was wet for some reason I didn't know. I looked down at my body. It was covered with bruises and scratch marks. My hands were tied behind my back. I could hear Max breathing not far from me but I couldn't see him since he was behind me. I tried to move but I was too sore to do a damn thing.

I woke up covered in sweat and tears. Charles was sound asleep. I was feeling sick so I just wrapped a sheet around my body and ran to the bathroom before I'd throw up on my bed. There wasn't much in my stomach but I threw up everything anyway.

"You're okay?" Charles asked as he walked into the bathroom in his boxers.

I was sitting on the bathroom floor. I just nodded but he knew me better than this to just leave. He sat by myside and wrapped his arm around my shoulders and pulled me in.

"Another nightmare?" he asked.

"Yeah!" I said weakly.

He held me for a while before we went back to bed. I took a pill to help me sleep this time. My head was exploding from the pain but I didn't take a painkiller, too. I thought if I could sleep, my headache would get better.

The next morning, I felt awful. My stomach hurt so much.

My headache has gotten even worse. And for some reason, my throat hurt, too. Charles wasn't in the bed but the smell of breakfast was coming from the kitchen. I tied my hair into a bun and took a shower before going to the kitchen. I thought I would take some coke before breakfast but I didn't. I took too much last night. I should control how much I take each day.

"Morning!" I said as I walked into the kitchen.

I leaned against the island and watched him. He was just wearing a pair of sweatpants.

"Morning babe!" he said and kissed me.

He was about to let go but I put my hand behind his neck and pulled him towards myself to kiss him properly.

"So, what's the occasion?" I asked as I let go of him.

"Nothing! Just thought you might be hungry," he said with a smile.

But it was not a happy smile. He knew something serious was wrong with me but he wouldn't ask too much. He asked a few times and I said I'm not ready to talk about it.

I couldn't look him in the eyes. I looked down to avoid any eye contact. We were quiet for a few minutes. I was feeling horrible. I needed an excuse to go back to my room to take some coke without making him suspicious.

"I'm going to get my phone. Do you want me to bring yours, too?" I said.

"I brought mine," he said.

I went back to my room and took some coke as fast as I could. My nose burned a little. I grabbed my phone and went back to the kitchen. I sat on the island and watched him making bacons, eggs and toasts. He poured me some coffee and gave it to me.

"Brooke? Your nose is bleeding!" he said in shock.

I couldn't even feel it. I jumped down from the island and ran to the bathroom. It wasn't much but still, I was bleeding. I knew this about coke but I didn't take that much to cause such thing. I cleaned it up and went back to the kitchen.

"Are you okay?" he asked.

"Yeah!" I said with a smile.

I didn't need to try too hard when I was high. Everything was good. Nothing hurt anymore. It felt like it was paradise on earth.

We ate in silence. Charles was deep in his thoughts and I was just happy. I helped him wash the dishes. I sat on the island as we were finished.

"So, how long have you known about Charlotte and James?" he asked as he leaned back against the counter.

"It's been a few days," I said with a smile.

"Why didn't you tell me?" he asked.

"I didn't have any right to tell you! Okay, you're her brother but she trusted me enough after like a day to tell me her secret. I couldn't betray her trust," I said.

"But still, James? I still can't believe it," he said.

"Yeah! I never thought I would ever see him call someone his girlfriend. I mean he's always been a player. He must really like Charlotte to stop messing around for her," I said.

"Yeah! But still James?" he said again.

"Are you worried about her?" I asked.

"Yeah! I mean it's James we're talking about!" he said.

"He was a player not a rapist," I said with laughter.

As soon as I said it, I regretted it. But Charles didn't get suspicious. Maybe it was because I was laughing. It always hurt to even say the word 'rapist' but not now, I couldn't feel a thing.

"You're right!" he said and came closer.

"Don't worry. Look at it like this. You're dating his little sister, he's dating yours," I said and pulled him closer with my legs.

"But he knows I wouldn't hurt you," he said.

"He wouldn't hurt her either," I said.

"He's better not," he said seriously.

I wrapped my legs around his waist and locked him in. He put his hands on my thighs and slid them to my waist. My hands were still on the island. He slid down his hands down to my hips and under my T-shirt. I put my hands on his bare shoulders and slid one to his hair and the other one to his back.

I looked into his eyes. They become more gray than green. I pulled him in and kissed him. In a few seconds, our tongues were wrapped around each other. His hand went higher on my back. His hand slipped under the strap of my bra. I pulled his hair a little. I kissed his neck a few times and went down to his chest. He let out a deep breath under my touch.

He was holding me by my hips tightly. His nails were going in my skin. He wouldn't let go. I came back up and kissed his lips. I was holding him as close as possible. We were kissing for a while before he'd picked me suddenly and took me to my bedroom. He sat on the bed with my on his lap. He took off my T-shit so fast.

"I thought I'd never see you in a bra!" he said with a smirk.

He kissed between my breasts. I pushed him on the bed and got on top of him. His hands were on my thighs while I was kissing him. I got up and took off my shorts. As soon as I got on top of him, he took off my bra. He grabbed me by my waist and laid me on the bed. He wasn't playing like last night.

He knew what he wanted. He knew what I wanted.

He slid down my panties and then took off his boxers. He grabbed a condom and put it on. As he got on me, I spread my legs wide open. He kissed me and thrusted into me swiftly. I let out a sigh as he entered me. I wrapped my legs around him and keep him as close as possible.

My moans got louder as he moved in and out faster. His lips didn't leave my lips and neck. His hands were by my head, keeping his weight a little off of me. My hands were on his back. I think my nails left marks on his back. I moaned out loud as I came. He went for a little longer till he came, too. He pulled out of me and covered us with a sheet. I crawled into his arms and rested my head on his chest.

His eyes were closed but he was awake. I couldn't stop wondering if I really deserved him or not? I'm keeping everything from him. He doesn't know a damn thing that's going on in my life. What would he do if I told him about Max? What would he do if he knew I was raped? What would he do if he knew I was taking coke? Wouldn't he leave me? I wouldn't blame him if he did.

He was the best thing that ever happened to me. He knew me. He knew my past, mostly. He was making my future. He knew what he was capable of. He could burn me to ash and recreate me like a phoenix. He could burn me with his love but he couldn't burn me with the cold. I was falling in love with him so fast that I couldn't even enjoy the ride. I was falling so hard that I was worried about hurting both of us.

Did I really deserve him? He was a pure angle and I was just a messed-up girl. I was too broken to be fixed. He was fixing everything in my life but could he fix this too? I don't think so! It was all on me to fix. I had to find a way to get better if I want to live. Did I want to live? About a year ago, no, I didn't. But now, he was my reason to live. He was my reason to get better. I had to get better. I had to get better, no matter what it takes.

Chapter Twenty

Days, weeks and months passed and everything has gotten even more complicated. Well, it's been about two months. Actually, a few days more than two months. What day it is? It's funny. It's my accident's anniversary. Heh! Anniversary! It's supposed to be something happy, isn't it? This one's more like a funeral. But I don't feel a damn thing. I'm so high I can't feel anything.

It's been two months and four days since the New Year's. It's March Fourth. It's funny how I remember everything now. Even the things I wasn't good at before.

Since the New Year's so many things happened. Charles and I got so much closer, especially physically. The new semester has started. I don't really work anymore. I started a painting but I didn't finish it. I was busy drinking and having fun with my friends. Charles and James talked me into playing the piano again.

Charles and I were spending most our time together. I think he's too worried about me to leave me alone. Well, can you blame him? I'm so messed up. He saw my nose bleed so many times now that he might think I have some sort of cancer. But then he noticed the way I'm losing weight. I think he's smart enough to know that I'm taking coke.

He asked me a few times if I wanted to talk about it but he got the same answer every single time. I always said that I wasn't ready to talk about it. I really wasn't. Even when I was supper high, I couldn't talk about it. Maybe I was too scared to tell him the truth. I was falling in love with him so hard that I couldn't afford to lose him.

On Valentine's Day, he took me on a fancy date and then we came back to my place. He played me a song and I heard him sing for the first time. I've heard him sing along with songs before but this was different. His voice was so beautiful, I could listen to him forever. Then we decided to watched *Titanic*. We stayed up till the sunrise and talked. It was just so nice and romantic. He was looking at me like I was the only girl in the whole world. I wished I'd be the only girl for him.

On the night of my birthday, Charles surprised me with a little party in his apartment. He even invited my few friends that I was still in touch with. Charlotte and Christian were there too. Christian had broken up with his girlfriend so he was all alone again. I introduced him to one of my old friends, Caroline. She wasn't a school friend. Our parents were friends so we knew each other since we were little. They spent the night talking to each other, and now they're dating.

Charlotte and James wouldn't leave each other's side for a second. I was happy for them. They were both happy and I was even happier because James had finally found someone who he'd finally stop sleeping around for. Even though Charlotte was about three years younger than him, nobody would notice that. She wasn't just an eighteen years old high school girl. She was a grown woman. Her brothers most be proud of her.

And Charles, he was the most amazing thing in that room. He was charming, gentle, kind, loving and everything a woman could ever ask for her lover to be. I wanted to tell him how much I loved him that night but as soon as I opened my mouth, I choked. He hasn't said it yet but I wanted to be the first one to say it. He was becoming my whole world.

I know! I'm talking like a nineteenth century woman who's looking for a husband. But he was the only thing I wanted right now in the whole world. I tried a few times to quit cocaine but I couldn't. I was thinking of going to rehab in the summer. Why not sooner? Well, I can't miss my classes. Or even worse, I could get suspended from school. I couldn't do that to my future.

I started my therapy again. It's not helping me much but it's keeping me from using too much coke. Yes! I told my therapist that I was taking coke. She freaked out at first but then told me how to use it and when to use it. She wasn't really happy about it but she helped me not to overdose.

Charles knew I was seeing my therapist again. He thought she could help me with my nightmares but she really couldn't. I tried to sleep without pills but it just led me to another nightmare and waking up in the middle of the night and throwing up.

I really wanted to get better but nothing could make the nightmares go away except for the pills. Not even coke. Yes, I tried that, too! Charles was worried about me and how I was taking so many medications. I could see it in his eyes. But still, he wouldn't say anything. He'd just wake up and hold my hair and rub my back every time I'd waken up in the middle of the night.

Sometimes I felt like he feels like he's babysitting me. But still every time I apologized to him for waking him up at three in the morning, he'd always say 'Never say that again!' and kiss my forehead. Wasn't he the perfect man? If he wasn't the perfect man who would be?

It's been more than two months that we were dating and I knew him better than myself. He knew me pretty well, too. Except for the fact that I was raped and I was taking coke every single day. We exchanged keys about two weeks ago. It was soon in a normal relationship but we were practically living together. Either he was here or I was at their place.

I'd see Charlotte every now and then. She talked to her dad after the New Year's party since he saw James kissing her. She would spend the weekends there with James. Charles and I tried to stay those nights at my place so they could have a little privacy. And it was a little weird for Charles to spend the night with James. He was still worried about her. Well, I wouldn't blame him. I was more worried about Charlotte than I was worried about James.

It's Friday and I didn't have any classes so I stayed home. Charles had a class in the morning and had to go to the office afterward. I spent the morning cleaning up my apartment. I was just lying on the couch, trying not to take any coke as long as I possibly could. It didn't last that long. I took some but it didn't do a damn thing so I took some more.

As it burned my nose, I waited a few minutes to see if I needed more or not. I needed more. So, I took some more and just laid on the couch and enjoyed my time. I decided it was time to tell Charles everything. I needed to tell him that I was raped. I needed to tell him that I was taking cocaine. And most importantly, I needed to tell him I loved him.

I laughed out loud at my thoughts. I couldn't tell him that. Could I? Wouldn't he leave me? No! He wouldn't leave me! He wouldn't leave a broken girl like me right on the anniversary of her drunken accident. He was an angle. He wouldn't leave me.

So, I grabbed my phone and called him. He must have been in a meeting because he sent me straight to voice mail. Normally I would just hang up and he would call me back but I was too high. I wanted to tell him everything before I could change my mind.

Chapter Twenty-One

It's been about three months since we started dating. We were closer to each other than ever. But still Brooke was hiding something from me. She was losing weight. She acted like nothing could hurt her but still she couldn't sleep without pills. She was seeing her therapist again but she wouldn't tell me why. I asked about it a few times and all I got was 'I'm not ready to talk about it!'. But when would she be ready?

I watched her carefully for the past month or so. The way her nose bleeds every now and then could be the sign of two very different things and I was afraid of them both. It was either she was taking cocaine or she had cancer. But the way she was losing weight was telling me she was taking coke. I wanted to confront her but every time I tried, I failed.

It was Friday and I had a class in the morning and a meeting so I came to the office. I was too distracted at the meeting that it took twice the time it should've taken. My phone rang in the middle of the meeting and it was Brooke. I just sent her straight to voicemail. It was the code that I was in a meeting or a class.

She'd always hang up but she left a voicemail this time. I didn't know why but I felt my heart dropped in my chest. She left a five-minute message. She must have needed to tell me something important. I excused myself out of the meeting and went back to my office. I was too scared to press play but I did it anyway.

"Hi babe! I know it's weird that I'm leaving you a voicemail but I thought if I didn't tell you now, I wouldn't tell you in months. I think you should know the truth. I got my memories back! I remember what exactly led me to my accident. Charles, babe, I was raped on the night of my eighteenth birthday by my dear fiancé who is now dead thanks to my dad! There is more. I'm taking coke! I'm actually so high right now! I can't feel a thing. It's awesome. And last but not least, I love you, Charles. I love you, Charles. You…" she said.

The next thing I heard was a loud bump and then nothing. The voicemail went for about another minute and I heard nothing. I couldn't shake the feeling that she might have overdosed. She said she saw so high. I grabbed my keys and got out of my office.

"Jack. Tell them I had to go. We'll continue the meeting another time." I told my assistant as I was running to the elevator.

I called nine-one-one as I was starting my car in the parking. I told them she might have overdosed on cocaine and gave them her address. It was taking me too long to get to her apartment. So, I called James to go there.

"Hey! What's up?" he said as he picked up.

"James, listen to me. There a good chance that Brooke has overdosed. Please go there," I said.

"What do you mean she might have overdosed?" he asked confused.

"She's taking coke in case you haven't notice," I said.

"Okay! I'm on my way!" he said and hung up.

He had a key to her apartment. She didn't know that but I

made a key to her apartment for him. I was glad I did that behind her back. I was worried sick. I got stuck in the traffic. It took me more than half an hour to get there.

When I got to her apartment, there was an ambulance in front of her building. I parked my car and ran upstairs. James was already there. They were putting her on a stretcher. They took her out the apartment. James was standing there with tears in his eyes.

"What happened to her?" I asked.

"They said she might have had a heart attack," he said trying to hold back tears.

I couldn't say a word. Before we left the apartment, I noticed something on the coffee table, a card and some white powder in a small plastic bag. My heart ached at the sight. I couldn't believe she was doing this to herself.

We locked the door and left the apartment. We went to the hospital and waited to get some answers. I couldn't sit still. I was pacing back and forth in the hallways trying to figure out everything she said on the phone.

"Charles, you got to sit down," James said after about half an hour.

"I can't James. I can't! What if she doesn't make it?" I asked.

I didn't want to believe something might happen to her but what if?

"She will make it. She got through way worse than this. She will make it," James said.

"Did you know she got her memories back?" I asked.

It didn't shock him but he looked away. He knew? What the hell? Did he know she got raped? I was shocked, angry and confused. I sat down before I'd pass out.

"You knew?" I asked in shock.

"Yeah," he said quietly.

"Why didn't you say something? You knew she was going through hell and didn't tell me?" I asked.

"She wasn't ready to tell you. You know she would've told you if she was ready," he said.

I couldn't believe it. Was she ready to talk to him about it and she wasn't ready to talk to me, to her own boyfriend? It hurt me a little at first but as I thought about it more, I didn't blame her anymore. Her last two boyfriends were horrible people. On raped her and the other cheated on her and robbed her.

I put my head on my hands and ran my fingers through my hair. It was too much, even for me. I couldn't imagine what she went through this whole time. I was going crazy even thinking about it. I loosened my tie to get some proper air. I got up and walked the hallway from end to end. James left and came back with two cups of coffee. I sat again.

"What else didn't she tell me? She said her ex is dead thanks to her father! Is it true?" I asked.

I was afraid to hear the answer but still, I had to know what led her to a possible heart attack even if it meant I was about to hear the most terrifying thing I have ever heard.

"What exactly did she tell you?" he asked worried.

I gave him my phone to listen to the voicemail she left me. He listened carefully. I wished she said everything. I couldn't take any more than this. It was already too much. He handed me my phone but before he could say anything, a nurse came and told us that she's stable and we can see her.

As we went to her room, I felt a huge pain in my chest. I never thought I'd see her like this. The woman I loved with all of my heart was now laying on a hospital bed, attached to a heart monitor and an oxygen mask on her face.

The tears I tried to hold back earlier, streamed down my face. I didn't dare to go any closer. I didn't want to believe it was actually real. I wanted to wake up beside her and hold her tight and never let go.

But it was not a nightmare. It was real. Brooke was laying on the bed unconscious. She didn't look anything like the girl I met three months ago, before she got her memories back. She looked thinner and weaker. There were no signs of that wonderful strong woman in her anymore.

I blamed myself for not taking better care of her, for not putting pressure on her to tell me what was going on. I blamed myself for not asking her why she was taking coke when I was a hundred present sure she was on drugs. I was a coward.

"What do you want to know?" James asked after a few minutes of silence.

"Everything!" I said.

"So, you'd better sit down," he said and we both sat down.

"Do you remember the night of the court when we went to her apartment and Ben came too?" he asked and I just nodded.

"Do you remember when he found out she couldn't remember anything for about a month before her accident?" he asked and I nodded.

"That night he was saying things like it was all his fault and if he had come back, it wouldn't have happened. He didn't say what wouldn't have happened. I thought he was just shocked or something. A few days after that, the day before Christmas, she called me from the hospital to pick her up but I didn't ask what was going on. I just picked her up and took her to her apartment. When I asked her what was going on, she said she remembered everything. Her fiancé raped her on the night of her eighteenth birthday. And ten days later, she drank a bottle of wine and drove to her ex's house or at least she wanted to and she gets into an accident," he said and took a deep breath before saying more.

"But the thing is, Ben didn't come back for her birthday. She called him the day after her birthday and told him everything. He knew what happened to her this whole time and blamed himself for it. I went to see Ben after I left her place. Apparently, she wanted to tell her father what happened but he just walked out on her," he said.

I couldn't believe it. It was too much to get in a few minutes. My head was already exploding but there was more to the story.

"I couldn't take it. Ben was going insane and her father knew he couldn't live with this so we did what we had to do. We dug up everything we could about him. And Logan killed his best friend's son with his own hands," he said.

"Why are you keep saying fiancé?" I asked after a few minutes.

"She was supposed to marry him some day. They were engaged then," he said.

I couldn't believe it. I couldn't take it. It was too much even for me just to hear. I couldn't imagine what Brooke went through. I got up and walked around the room for a few minutes.

"Why didn't she tell me anything?" I asked, afraid to hear the answer.

"She wanted to figure it out on her own first but then she was too afraid to lose you. She didn't want to drag you into this mess," he said.

"But exactly how?" I asked.

I was sad, upset and terrified to lose her for real. What would happen if I didn't listen to her voicemail? What would happen if she didn't leave a message and hung up as always?

"Charles, she loved you more than you could ever imagine," he said with tears in his eyes.

"Don't you think I love her just as much? But now I might never get the chance to tell her that," I said as I was crying.

There was no point of holding back my tears. I learned the most hurtful truths about the love of my life and what led her here.

"You will tell her how much you love her. I promise you. She went through hell and came back. She'll get through this, too," he said.

I wanted to believe him but the thought of never telling her how much I loved her was killing me. I needed to keep calm. I needed to be here for her.

I sat by her bed and held her hand in mine and kissed it. I couldn't help my tears. They just streamed down my face. I didn't even bother to wipe them. I didn't want to let go of her hand. James left and came back with her doctor after a while.

"Charles? This is Doctor Benson. He's been her doctor since last year," he said.

I wiped my tears and shook his hand.

"How is she?" I asked terrified to hear the answer.

"Well, I don't have much good news. She overdosed with cocaine. We don't know how long she'll be in a coma..." He said but I cut him off.

"She's in a coma?" I asked as I was trying to hold back my tears.

I don't know what I was expecting but hearing that she was in a coma from her doctor was a whole another level of painful.

"Unfortunately, yes. Maybe if the ambulance got there a few minutes earlier, she wouldn't be in a coma now. There was about two grams of cocaine in her system which is a lot. We ran a few tests. The results should be back soon. We'll know more then," he said.

I couldn't say a word. He left after checking on Brooke and I just stood there staring into nothing. It couldn't be true, could it? I sat beside her bed and held her hand again. I wanted to believe she would wake up eventually but what if she didn't? How was I supposed to live without her? It's been only a few hours and I already felt like my heart would stop any second.

Chapter Twenty-Two

"Charles?" James said as he came back after a few hours.

As I looked up, I saw the last people I'd want to see right now, Brooke's parents. I didn't like to admit it but he looked ten years older since Christmas but his wife looked the same. I guessed he didn't tell her or she didn't care at all.

"Thank you, Charles, for taking care of her. We'll stay if you like to go home," he said.

"I'm not leaving her alone with you, ever!" I said straight forward.

James got shocked. I'm usually more polite but I couldn't take it anymore. Her father didn't get so shocked. He must have expected it. But her mother was clearly shocked.

"Charles, dear, you can go home. We can stay with her," she said with a sad smile.

"Why would I ever leave her in your hands again? I wasn't there last year but now, now I'm not going to leave her in the hands that led her here, in this fucking hospital in the first place," I said with rage.

He looked down but her mother was still confused.

"What are you talking about dear?" she asked.

"Didn't you tell her what happened to her daughter?" I asked.

I was angrier than ever. He just looked away and didn't say a word.

"Wow! You really didn't tell her?" I asked.

She looked more confused than before. I was too angry to be delicate or polite. I blamed them. I blamed myself. I blamed everyone for this horrifying situation.

"What didn't you tell me Logan?" she asked.

"Your daughter was assaulted on the night of her birthday last year. That was the reason she was driving drunk and got into that car crash. But she couldn't remember it until two months ago. And when she got her memories back, she remembered that when she wanted to tell her dear old dad, he walked out on her," I said.

My hands got numb from fisting them too tight. I couldn't do or say anything else. She was shocked. All she could do was to stare at her husband and hope to hear it was just a stupid joke.

"Is it true?" she asked as tears streamed down her eyes.

As her husband nodded, she couldn't breathe anymore. James left the room and came back with a bottle of water. He helped her to sit down. She cried for a while. I couldn't do anything. I didn't want to do anything. Logan has left the room and left us with his wife. James held her till she calmed down.

"Why was she taking coke?" she asked.

"I'm not sure but I guess she took it to feel less. It was all too much for her. And on top of it all, I really don't think that bastard's death did her any good!" I said more calmly.

"How did you even find out she, you know, overdosed?" she asked

She was standing by her bed, staring at her daughter.

"She called me and left a voicemail which was odd so I listen to it and she was saying that she was high and the next thing I heard was a loud bump," I said as I tried not to cry.

He came back after a while but still didn't say anything. He just stood there by the door, watching her from a distance. They stayed a little longer and then left.

I didn't even know what time it was. All I knew was that I was so tired and I didn't want to sleep. I couldn't sleep.

"Charles, you should rest a little. You've been here for hours! You haven't even eaten a bite. Go home. I'll stay here with her," James said.

"I don't want to rest. I want to be here, with her," I said and sat by her bed.

"How about this? You go home, change and eat something and come back and stay the night here, with her," he said.

I could see the tears in his eyes. It was maybe even harder for him to see her like this. He knew her for almost his entire life but I knew her for like three months. If I could fall for her in three months, he would love her even more than I did.

"Okay!" I said.

"Give me your car keys," he said as I was leaving.

"Why?" I asked.

"Because you're not in any shape to drive. I can't have you on one these beds, too," he said.

He was right. I wasn't in a good shape. I gave him my keys and left. I didn't take a cab either, I walked to our place. I needed some fresh air. I walked for about fifteen minutes till I got to our apartment. As I closed the door, I let my tears fall down my face. I couldn't hold them back anymore. Why would I hold them back anyway? The woman of my dreams was laying on a hospital bed.

I took a shower after a while, and wore something more comfortable than the suit I was wearing earlier. I grabbed my charger, my headphones and my guitar. I tuned my guitar, before going back to the hospital. I packed some clean clothes, too. I knew I wouldn't leave there before she wakes up. I didn't care if I had to drop my semester. I didn't want to leave her there alone or with anybody else. I wanted to be there every single second of every single day.

I walked back to the hospital. As I went up to her room, it was empty. I felt my heart dropped in my chest. I grabbed my phone and called James.

"James? What happened? Where's Brooke?" I asked, scared to hear the answer.

"Hey! I was about to call you. They transferred her to another room," he said.

He gave me the room number. It didn't take me long to get there. It was on a higher floor. As I got there, the nurses and the doctors were leaving. As everyone left, it was only James, Doctor Benson and I. I was too worried to hear any kind of news right now except that she will wake up soon. I just hoped for the best as he started to speak.

"Well, the results are better than I thought they would be. Her organs are perfectly fine. The only thing I'm a little worried about is her memories. We can't say anything for sure right now but since she lost her memories once and her body was deoxygenated for about ten minutes, she might suffer from memory loss again!" Doctor Benson said.

I was too shocked to say anything. James thanked him and he left. She might lose her memory again? She might not remember me? Did it really matter? I just wanted her to wake up. I didn't care if she didn't remember me. I just wanted to look into her eyes, her beautiful brown eyes and tell her how much I loved her, even if she couldn't remember a thing about me.

"Did you eat?" James asked after a while.

"No! I wanted to come back as soon as possible," I said and sat by her bed.

"Okay! I'll be back," he said and left.

I didn't dare to talk to her. It felt like I was accepting the fact that she might stay unconscious for a while. I held her hand in mine and kissed it. Her hand was cold as always. I liked how her hands were always cold. It was my excuse to hold them in mine and warm them up.

I fell asleep on that chair with her hand in mine. James woke me after about half an hour. He brought food and some snacks so I wouldn't starve myself. He knew I couldn't eat much when I was worried about something.

"You got to eat something, Charles," he said as I was playing with my food.

"I can't eat!" I said.

"Charles, you're not helping her getting better or waking up any sooner! You're starving yourself just like you did a few months ago over your meeting with her and the concert," he said.

I could say he was worried about me but I couldn't eat. After an hour of playing with my food, I could eat a little. James stayed for a little longer. It was pretty late. I didn't want to sleep but I had too. I kissed her forehead before going to sleep on the couch that was in her room. I would wake up every few hours but she was still unconscious.

Days passed by one by one. Each day someone would come to see her. Her father didn't come again but her mother came every day to see her. James would come in once in the morning and once in the evening. He would make sure I ate that day. He brought Charlotte a few times with himself but I really wished he didn't. She cried a lot each time she came. Christian came once with them.

Ben came back to New York the day after she overdosed. He came a few times with his mother. He was still blaming all of this on himself and himself only. It was kind of his fault but he really had to stop beating himself up over it. Her parents had responsibilities, too. I couldn't stop thinking about what would happen if her father didn't walk out on her? What would happen then? Would she be safe and sound right now?

I would play her some of her favorite songs on the guitar and the ones I couldn't I just put headphones on her ears and played them for her. She hasn't moved a finger or made any signs of consciousness but I wouldn't give up any time soon.

It's been a week. She gained a little weight. Her face look like before she started taking coke. But she looked so pale. She looked so weak. She was my everything and I was just sitting here hoping I could hold her again and tell her how much I love her.

I grabbed my guitar and started to play and sing for her. I really wasn't into singing but she liked it. So, I would sing for her. After a few songs, I remember a song I played her on Valentine's Day. It was a few years old but she loved it. So, I decided to play her the song.

"From the way you smile to the way you look
You capture me unlike no other
From the first hello, yeah, that's all it took
And suddenly we had each other
And I won't leave you
Always be true
One plus one, two for life
Over and over again.

So, don't ever think I need more
I've got the one to live for
No one else will do, and I'm telling you
Just put your heart in my hands
Promise it won't get broken
We'll never forget this moment
Yeah, we'll stay brand-new 'cause I'll love you
Over and over again
Over and over again.

From the heat of night to the break of day
I'll keep you safe and hold you forever
And the sparks will fly, they will never fade
'Cause every day gets better and better
And I won't leave you
Always be true
One plus one, two for life
Over and over again.

So, don't ever think I need more
I've got the one to live for
No one else will do, yeah, I'm telling you
Just put your heart in my hands
I promise it won't get broken
We'll never forget this moment
Yeah, we'll stay brand-new 'cause I'll love you
Over and over again
Over and over again.

Girl, when I'm with you I lose track of time

When I'm without you you're stuck on my mind
Be all you need till the day that I die
I'll love you
Over and over again.

So, don't ever think I need more
I've got the one to live for
No one else will do, yeah, I'm telling you
Just put your heart in my hands
Promise it won't get broken
We'll never forget this moment
Yeah, we'll stay brand-new 'cause I love you
Over and over again
Yeah, over and over again."

Over and over again. I sang as tears were running down my face.

"Why are you crying?"

I heard a weak voice after a few minutes. As I looked up, I saw her eyes, her big beautiful eyes. I couldn't believe it. She was awake.

Chapter Twenty-Three

"Why are you crying?" she asked again.

I couldn't say a word. I just put my guitar down and got up. Her eyes followed my every move. She was awake. She woke up. Tears streamed down my face faster. I bent down and kissed her forehead.

"You're awake!" I said as I wiped my tears.

She just smiled at me and reached for her mask to took it off.

"You're awake!" I said.

I was too afraid it would be just another dream. She reached and wiped my tears.

"You're awake!" I said again.

"I'm awake!" she said.

Her smile was more beautiful than ever. She was smiling with all of her heart and soul. I've missed how she smiled like there was nothing important in the world. I started laughing and called for doctors to come check on her. They transferred her to another room to do a few tests on her. The first thing I did was calling James and Ben that she woke up. They both said they'd come right away.

I looked horrible. I took a quick shower and shaved. I didn't want her to see me like this. I was a mess. And by mess I meant I looked like a homeless man. I haven't showered in days. The last time I shaved was before she overdosed.

James and Ben arrived a little before they brought her back. They said she could leave in forty-eight hours. Well, if everything goes well! Fortunately, she didn't lose her memories again and remembered everything. She said she was okay but deep down, even she didn't believe it. She couldn't pretend like before. What was the point of hiding it when all of us knew what she's been through?

Her parents came. She wasn't so happy about it. But still she didn't say anything to upset them. I didn't call Charlotte or Christian. Well, I forgot, but James called them! They came with a pink and white rose bouquet. Charlotte couldn't stop crying. She cried a lot in the past week.

It was like a little party. She was laughing. It wasn't a dream this time. She was awake and fine. There was nothing attached to her any more. I went back to her place to bring her some clean clothes while others were with her.

As I walked in her apartment my heart dropped in my chest. The moment when they were taking her out of there on the stretcher flashed before my eyes. There was dust everywhere. There was still some coke on the coffee table. Before I get her some clean clothes, I got rid of the coke and cleaned the coffee table. I didn't want her to come back and face this scene.

I grabbed her some comfortable clothes and a cute outfit and put them in a bag. She wanted to take a shower so I grabbed her shampoo and hair oil and other stuff. She didn't know it yet but the news of her overdose got out before her father or I could do anything. As I went back to the hospital, her parents had left but the others were still there. She was sitting on her bed, laughing out loud as I walked in.

She could eat and do whatever she wanted to do but she

had to stay in the hospital so if anything happened, they could help her immediately. I really hoped nothing would happen to her.

"You shaved!" she said as we were finally alone.

"Yeah!" I said with a little smile.

I knew she didn't like facial hair. She preferred a clean face.

"So, what did you bring me?" she asked.

"I brought you some comfortable clothes and an outfit for the day after tomorrow!" I said.

She still had a little problem walking since she was still for a week. So, I helped her go the bathroom to take a shower. As she was in the shower, James brought us some food and left before she came out. She must be really hungry. She hasn't eaten anything since she woke up.

She came out of the shower all cleaned up. She's wrapped her hair in a towel. She looked so pretty. I could stare at her for hours and not get tired. We sat on the couch and ate our dinner.

"So, anything interesting happened while I was unconscious?" she asked as she was eating.

"I really don't know what was happening outside of this room," I said quietly.

"Don't tell me you've been here all this time!" she said shocked.

"Where would I be?" I asked.

She didn't say anything. A tear dropped on her cheek. I wiped it right away.

"So, you've been here for the past week?" she asked to make sure.

I just nodded. I really couldn't get a word out of my

mouth.

"How did you, you know, found out I, umm, overdosed?" she asked.

"You left me a voicemail which was unusual. So, I listened to it right away and then I heard a loud bump. And you were saying you were so high," I said but she stayed quiet.

"Brooke, promise me you'll never keep anything from me," I said after a few minutes.

"Can I not?" she said.

"Brooke, I cannot see you like this ever again. I know I'm being selfish but I can't. I know it must've been so hard for you to go through this all by yourself. But I want to be there for you. I can't let you do this to yourself again," I said.

I really couldn't. I don't know what would happen if she wouldn't wake up for another week. I was already going insane. If anything happened to her again, I would lose my mind. I could go insane.

"Okay! I promise," she said.

"Thank you!" I said.

As we finished our dinner, we laid on the couch, cuddling. I was playing with her hair, thinking I should tell her or not. I waited too long last time.

"Brooke?" I said and she turned around to face me.

"I love you! I love you Miss. Edwards," I said.

She didn't say anything. She just put her hands on my face and kissed me. I was too afraid to believe I might never kiss her again. But there she was, kissing me. I put my hands on her waist and pulled a little up. I wanted her, all of her but I thought it would be better if we waited 'til she was released from the hospital.

"I love you Mister Charles Young," she said as she let go.

She was pretty tired so she went to sleep sooner than I did. I didn't know how to tell her that she's been in the headlines for the last week and she might be the headline of every single newspaper tomorrow and the day after that. I couldn't hide it from her. She would find out sooner or later. I was about to go to sleep when my phone rang. It was Logan Edwards. I got out of the room to pick up.

"Hello?" I said as I picked up.

"Charles? This is Logan Edwards," he said.

"Yes, I know! How can I help you?" I asked.

I tried to be polite but my voice was stone cold. I couldn't forgive him for what he did to Brooke.

"I just wanted to thank you for all you've done for my daughter," he said.

"No problem. I'm just happy she's finally awake," I said.

"You're a good guy. She's lucky she has you. Goodbye," he said and hung up.

It was so weird. I have never seen or heard him like this. He didn't come over this past week. He just came today. I didn't know why. Probably because the way I acted on the first day.

I couldn't sleep for like an hour. I couldn't stop thinking about Brooke and her father. What would happen if he didn't walk out on her? What would happen if she hasn't driven drunk? What would happen if she didn't start to paint? What would happen if she didn't leave home? Would she still go to NYU? Would she still be with me?

Everything that made us closer and closer wouldn't even happen. She wouldn't get robbed and I wouldn't help her. Even though she might have still run into James and might even hung out with us that night and help us for the concert.

But would James tell me about her before we'd even see her in the halls? I heard her name in James' stories but not much before she put up her exhibitions.

There were so many ifs in my head I didn't want to think about. Because with every if came the possibility of us not even meeting and I really didn't want to think about it. I just wanted to be with her from now on. I didn't want to leave her side. I wanted to help her get through this. It didn't matter how much time it would take us. I will help her get through this. I will help her get well. I want to make her happy.

I didn't care if it took six months, a year or even more. I wanted to give her a reason to want to get better without drugs or heavy medications. I wanted to be that reason.

Chapter Twenty-Four

The day of her release came eventually. She couldn't wait to get out of the hospital and go straight home. But still, I couldn't tell her about the headlines. I was right. She was the headline of most newspapers in New York that day. I had to talk to her about it before she walks out of the hospital and see a sea of paparazzi. She would get traumatized. She was ready to go. All the paperwork was done. I called my dad's driver to pick us not only because there were so many people out of the hospital but also because James still wouldn't let me drive.

"Brooke? I think you should know something before we leave," I said.

"Why are you saying it like that?" she asked.

"Well, the thing is the news of you know, what happened got out before your father or I could stop it. And now a bunch of paparazzi are outside," I said, trying to be careful with my words.

"It's okay. I thought it might've gotten out," she said with a smile.

She was trying to put on a brave face but she was scared. She's been struggling with death while others were talking about her overdose and why she was taking drugs.

As we walked out of the hospital, they were shouting out her name and asking questions. Neither Brooke nor I said a single word. If she decided to talk about what happened, she could do it later. We got in the car as soon as we could and got out of there.

"I didn't know my life was this interesting for people," she said sarcastically.

"People always love a good story," I said with a smirk.

She was one of those who experienced a lot before the age of twenty. She was only nineteen years old and had been in a coma twice now. She's been through a lot more than most people might have to go through in their entire lives.

"Home sweet home!" she said as she walked in her apartment.

It was just like when she left it. Even her phone was still on the ground. She grabbed it and plugged it in since it had run out of battery. She was acting like nothing has happened when it definitely had. I was scared for her, for myself.

"So, what do you want to do?" I asked.

"I just want to order a pizza and lay in my bed and watch a movie. But first I want to take a shower and get rid this hospital smell," she said with a smile.

So, we did what she wanted. She took a shower and I ordered a pizza and cleaned the place a little. It was almost clean but there was dust everywhere. Well, it's been more than a week since she's been here.

As I was cleaning, I thought about all the things that happened here, all the things she's gone through in this apartment. Maybe it would be best if she moved out of here. I was thinking about moving out of my current apartment for a while now. Well, not a while. I started thinking about it since Charlotte told us she was dating James. It was kind of weird being there when they were together. I knew there's the possibility that she moves in with him soon.

I didn't want to accept that it might happen as she goes to college next semester. But it could happen. They were really happy with each other and I didn't want to break them up. For a minute I thought it might be a good idea if Brooke moved in with me. Well, not right now. I mean when I moved out into a new apartment.

"Charles?" Brooke called me and pulled me out of my thoughts.

"Yeah?" I said trying to pull my myself together.

"Are you okay?" she asked.

"Yeah, I was just thinking about some stuff," I said.

My thoughts were still all over the place. I pushed them aside to think about them later.

"The pizza's arrived. Should we eat in the bed or in the living room?" she asked.

"I don't know! I'm okay with both," I said.

We went to her bedroom and she put on a movie. I wasn't paying any attention to the movie. I didn't even catch the name. My head was filled with every possible scenario about me moving out and Brooke moving in with me. I wanted to take care of her, to help her get better. I wanted to see her smile like she would before, full of life and passion.

"Charles? Charles? Where are you?" Brooke asked and waved her hand in front of my face.

"I'm sorry. Did you say something?" I asked confused.

"Are you okay? You seem, I don't know, distracted," she said.

"No, I'm fine," I said.

I was trying to hide it but I couldn't. She knew me better than that. She knew when I wanted to hide something from her which I didn't do a lot.

"What's wrong, Charles?" she asked.

"It's nothing. You don't need to worry about it," I said and put a piece of her hair behind her ear.

"I don't need to worry about it? Charles, what's going on? You're not making me any less worried. Tell me what's going on!" She asked worried.

"I'm just worried about you, about being here again. I just cannot see you get hurt ever again," I said as I was looking down.

I didn't know if I was going too fast or not. I just wanted to make sure nothing's going to happen to her. I might appear as the strong guy but when it comes to my loved ones, I'm the most vulnerable guy in the world.

"What are you saying?" she asked.

I was a little worried to say it out loud but I thought it would be better if I told her.

"I was thinking it would be better if you moved somewhere else for a while," I said quietly.

She put her hand on my face and kissed me. I could feel her smile on my lips. As she put her other hand on my face and pulled me towards herself, I figure she didn't get mad at what I just said. I put my hands on her waist and pulled her towards myself and she sat on my lap.

"That's why I love you," she said as she pulled away.

"Actually, I was thinking about something else, too. What do you say we find a place together?" I said a little worried.

It was a really big step in any relationship and we were dating just for like three months now. I didn't want to do anything that would end our relationship but we were practically living together and I could take better care of her this way.

But the way the smile on her lips got bigger and bigger showed nothing but her approval. She gave me a kiss instead of answering. I thought she would let go after a couple of kisses but she didn't; she ran her fingers through my hair slowly and pulled me closer. My hands were still on her waist. She slid down her hands slowly to the bottom of my shirt and lifted it up as she was kissing me. She lifted it up until it was just below my arms. She leaned back a little and tried to take off my shirt but I didn't know if it was a good idea or not.

"Are you sure?" I asked.

"I barely could keep my hands off of you for the last two days," she said and kissed me again.

I wanted her just as much so I didn't argue with her. She took off my shirt and threw it somewhere on the floor. She ran her hands all over my chest and stopped on my shoulders. She pulled me in and kissed me passionately. She was still fully dressed. But after a couple of more kisses, she took off her shirt.

She was wearing a black laced bra underneath. She looked pretty hot in it. Before she could lean in again, I grabbed her waist and laid her on the bed and got on top of her. I kissed her down to her belly and then took off her tight yoga pants. She was wearing matching black laced panties underneath. She really wanted this to happen tonight.

I kissed her inner thighs before kissing her neck and lips again. She moaned under my kisses. As I was kissing her lips, she tried to take off my jeans. She unbuttoned it and pulled it down a little but she couldn't go far. As I was kissing her neck, she hooked her legs around mine and pulled me down. She pulled down my jeans a little more with her feet but not much.

She sighed in disappointment. I took off her bra and kissed between her breasts. She threw her head back as her nails were scratching my back at the same time. I got up and took off her panties slowly. As I kissed under her stomach, she moaned.

I couldn't take it anymore. I was pretty hard. I took off my jeans and put on a condom. I kissed her before I entered her. She moaned as I entered her. She threw back her head in pleasure. My head fell on her shoulder as I rocked back and forth. She was holding on my arms as I moved faster. I moved in and out till we both came.

As we came, I got out of her and laid beside her. She crawled into my arms and I covered us with a warm blanket. We stayed there in silence for a few minutes.

She got out of the bed and wore something more comfortable than what she was wearing before. She grabbed her laptop and came back to bed. We spent the rest of the night looking for apartments. She was thinking about renting a place since she already had her apartment but I was more thinking about buying.

We looked for both. We found a few apartments close to Central Park and it was close enough to the campus so we could walk there every morning. I honestly couldn't remember the last time I walked to the campus but it could be nice.

We slept around midnight but I woke up in the middle of the night. Brooke was shaking in my arms. She was covered in sweat. I woke her up. As she woke up, she ran to the bathroom and threw up. I followed her to the bathroom and held her hair back and rubbed her back.

"I'm sorry I woke you up again," she said as she was sitting on the bathroom floor.

"Come on, Brooke. You know I hate it when you say sorry for no reason," I said.

"Why do you even like me?" she said as tears ran down her face.

I wiped them right away and pulled her into my arms.

"First of all, I don't like you, I love you! And second of all, I love you because of you," I said and kissed her head.

"But I'm a mess!" she said.

"Would you just stop it? We'll figure this out together," I said.

"But I'm too broken," she said.

"Well, I like broken things," I said with a smirk.

"Why?" she asked confused.

"Because I can fix them, however I want," I said with a smirk and kissed her head again.

She washed her face and we went back to sleep. She could sleep till morning. I woke up a little before her so I made her breakfast and made her eat more than she usually eats. She needed to gain some weight. She's lost more than ten pounds by the looks of it. She was already thin and this weight loss made her too thin and pretty weak.

We spent the day looking for an apartment we both liked. We ended up renting an apartment close to Central Park since she like the view. It was already empty so we could move in right away. But there was a problem. I didn't get a chance to tell James that I was moving out. I knew he would be supportive but I was still nervous.

We were both pretty tired so we went back to her place so she could pick some stuff up. We decided to spent the night at our place with James and Charlotte. It wasn't the weekend but I knew she would be there. I called James as we decided to go there so we wouldn't surprise them.

I cooked and we spent the night talking. Brooke was still

pretty weak and couldn't stay up too late. She would get tired fast. And despite the fact that we've been out all day looking for an apartment, she didn't feel so tired.

"So, James. I think I should tell you something," I said before we would go to sleep.

"Don't tell me she's pregnant," he said with wide eyes.

"Actually, that was the second news," Brooke said with sarcasm.

Charlotte gasped and covered her mouth with her hand. She was looking at Brooke with wide eyes.

"I'm going to be an aunt?" she asked.

She tried not to laugh but as James opened his mouth to talk, she couldn't hold back any longer. There was a reason she wanted to be an actress.

"Oh, come on," James said with complaint.

"Actually, we're moving in together," I said.

Both James and Charlotte got shocked. They didn't say a thing for a few minutes.

"Congratulations but how exactly did it happen?" James asked.

"Well, we were both thinking it's better if I move out of my apartment and Charles suggested we could get a place together," Brooke said.

"Oh! Congratulations! So, when will you move out?" Charlotte asked with a smirk.

"Not so soon," I said with a serious *older brother* look.

She rolled her eyes since she knew I would move out as fast as I could.

It was getting late and Brooke was getting more tired so we went to sleep. She fell sleep within a few minutes. She wanted to take a pill so she wouldn't wake me up in the middle of the night but I didn't let her. I knew as long as she took the pills, she wouldn't get any better. And the more she took them, the less effective they'd become. I wanted to see her get better. I didn't want to see her numb herself with a bunch of pills again.

Chapter Twenty-Five

Days, weeks and months passed. Brooke got better and worse at first. The first month was the hardest. We moved into our apartment in a week. We both were going to our classes and didn't miss another session. It was Brooke's way to keep her mind as busy as possible. I wasn't sure how it would work at first.

In the first month we kept ourselves pretty busy. And since we moved in so fast, the apartment was a mess. We didn't know where most of our stuff was. The first thing we did was set up her studio so she could get back to her work. As I said, she kept herself as busy as she could to think less about everything.

After a few weeks, she put her apartment for sale. She really didn't want to set foot in that apartment ever again. She said it was too painful for her. But she had no idea it was even more painful for me to walk in there. I didn't tell her that but every time I walked in there, I'd just see her, being carried out on a stretcher. That apartment was where I kissed her for the first time but I couldn't stay there anymore, neither could she.

She had even more bad memories there. Yes, she had some fun there and it was the first place she bought for herself with her own money. But she's been there with Nick, the guy who was cheating on her all along and robbed her at the end. It was the place she overdosed in. Who would want to live in a place that they almost died in?

She got a place outside of the city. We would go there on the weekends with James, Charlotte, Christian and Caroline. Ben would come whenever he was in New York. His relationship with Brooke was getting better. She forgave him but she still wouldn't talk to her father. Her mother came to see us a few times. It was weird for Brooke to talk to her mother. They've never been close to each other.

I was trying my best to help her. She'd wake up most of the nights covered in sweat and crying. She'd throw up most of the nights. She gained a little weight back but then she started to lose weight again. So, I kept feeding her as much as I could. She wouldn't eat much when she was alone but when I was there, I'd make sure she would eat enough.

I'd wake up every morning a little sooner than her to make breakfast. Well, at first at least. She didn't buy it for long that I just woke up earlier and I decided to make breakfast. After a week or two, she'd wake up too and we'd make breakfast together. She'd eat breakfast the easiest so I tried to fill her breakfast with nutritious.

We've cut out our alcohol since it would make her even more sick at nights. Her therapist suggested that actually. Yes, she's going to therapy again but she's not taking any more medications. Even if she gets a headache, she wouldn't take a painkiller. It was a little hard at first to convince her to do but it got easier over time.

She's put on an amazing exhibition in June. I bought the number one before the exhibition would open up. I had all of her number ones till now. I didn't know why she would always put her best work in every collection for number one. The other numbers were pretty good too but the number ones were just something else.

After the exhibition the talk of her overdose started all over again. She ignored them for a couple of days but then decided to speak about it. She did an interview and told her whole story. She started on the night of her eighteenth birthday to the day she overdosed. I was there. She broke with every word she said. But she held herself together till the end. She cried a lot after the interview but in a few days, she started getting way better.

She's changed a lot since I met her for the first time. She was an independent woman who broke in front of my eyes. She turned from a strong woman to a traumatized girl. But she's not that broken girl anymore. She pulled herself back together. She's moved on with her life. Sure, it took about five months but it was all worth it. Because she doesn't have any nightmares anymore. She's better than ever. She's more focused than ever. She's heading to her goals and nothing can stop her.

Now I'm looking at the most beautiful woman in the whole world and I can't be more thankful for being with her. She's all I have ever wanted and more. She's kind, caring, unbelievably talented, smart and beautiful inside and out. She makes me want to be better and better every single day. She pushes me to go farther and never get scared of what might come my way. She brings out the best of me, the version of me that I didn't know it even existed.

For the past eight months, we've been through so many things that I've never thought I'd experience in a million years. But that's the amazing part of life. It always put you through things you have never expected, thing you would never choose for yourself to go through. But at the end of the day that's what make you who you are.

It all brought us to today, my twenty-second birthday. I'm with the love of my life. She's shining brighter than ever in her purple silk dress, with her smile bigger than ever as she's walking towards me with a cake in her hands.

"Make a wish!" she said as she put the cake in front of me.

I wished to never have to be apart from her, to spend the rest of my life with her. And then I blew the candles.

"What did you wish for?" she asked.

"They say if you say your wish out loud, it won't come true," I said with a smile.

"Do you really believe in that?" she asked.

"Yes, because now I have you," I said with a smile.

Last year I wished to meet her. I never though wishing to meet her would end me up with her the next year. But then again, that's the best part of life.

It was the best birthday party I have ever had, thanks to Brooke. She planed the whole thing and I didn't know there would be a party until last night. I thought even if I wanted, I couldn't ask for anything better than being with her.

I was having the best time with my friends and family. But every time I looked at her, I wondered, was tonight a good time to ask the question or not? I knew we haven't even been together for a year but I couldn't wait to know I'm going to spend the rest of my life with her.

The thought of it was kind of scary. Maybe she was too young to get serious with somebody. Maybe I was too young to get married. The thought of her rejecting me was the most terrifying thing in my life right now.

As everyone left and we were alone, I decided to ask her.

I was thinking about it for a few months now. I couldn't wait any longer.

"Babe?" I said as I found her in the living room.

"Yeah!" she said as she was cleaning.

She was still in her beautiful dress. I tapped her on the shoulder and she turned around. I got on one knee. She got confused as I knelt in front of her.

"Brooke Victoria Edwards, you are the love of my life. Over the past eight months we've been through a lot and it just made me fall in love with you more and more every single day. I can't imagine my life without you. Will you marry me?" I asked.

And I felt the time freezing. My heart was barely beating. She didn't move or say a thing. I was getting scared to hear her answer. But who knew what she'd say? Maybe it could be the beginning of something bigger, something bigger than us.